SHORT RIDES:
KING OF HEARTS,
ROUGH ROAD,
ALL KNOCKED UP

LORELEI JAMES

Short Rides: *King of Hearts, Rough Road, All Knocked Up
Lorelei James
Published by LJLA, LLC
Copyright 2013, LJLA LLC
Cover by Shawn Gross Photography
ISBN: 978-0-9888235-2-5

*King of Hearts previously published in Guns And Roses Anthology 2012

KING OF HEARTS

A Rough Riders short story, featuring Crook County Deputy Cam McKay, from *Shoulda Been A Cowboy*.

AUTHOR'S NOTE

This story takes place a few months after the end of *Cowboy Casanova,* Rough Riders book 12…

A murder/suicide.

In Sundance, Wyoming.

It was one of the worst scenes Deputy Cam McKay had dealt with. And he'd seen a lot of horrific things over the years. He'd served several rotations in Iraq and witnessed the aftermath of suicide bombers. He'd seen animals used as vessels to hold bombs. He'd been in a caravan that'd hit a string of IEDs, resulting in death and dismemberment of his fellow soldiers. He hadn't come away from war unscathed—he'd lost most of his left leg, part of his hand, and bore scars, both visible and invisible.

During his time as deputy in Crook County, he'd dealt with deadly car accidents, including a fatality involving his cousin, Luke McKay. He'd broken up domestic disputes where one or both of the parties were drunk, armed, angry, and bleeding. He'd stumbled across a wild horse slaughter.

But this? It was beyond sickening.

The hysterical 911 call from the neighbor who'd discovered the bodies hadn't prepared him at all for what he'd found at the crime scene.

His stomach roiled as his brain flashed back to the carnage and he fought the urge to throw up.

Again.

But Cam hadn't been alone in his reaction. Sheriff Shortbull had stumbled outside and heaved over the juniper hedge after his glimpse at the dead couple.

A murder/suicide.

In Sundance, Wyoming.

Happy Valentine's Day.

Maybe it seemed worse because Cam knew the couple. He'd graduated from high school with Jeff Wingate. Cam couldn't fathom how the mild-mannered insurance salesman could carry out such brutality, especially to his wife. And Angela hadn't fought back. She'd literally lay down and died.

What a fucking waste.

What a fucking mess.

There'd been no indication of domestic issues. No 911 phone calls in the last year. No history of violence. He'd seen them eating in Dewey's Delish Dish two weeks ago. They'd acted... happy.

Because the crime scene was beyond their small county's investigative expertise, they'd had to call in the DCI from Cheyenne. Which meant waiting for the crew to arrive. But neither Cam nor Sheriff Shortbull could stomach waiting inside the house where the bloodbath had occurred.

So they stood outside in the frigid February weather, taking turns warming up in their patrol cars. He and the sheriff were too disturbed to slide into their usual defense mechanism, cracking jokes—which was how most law enforcement officers handled unpleasant aspects of the job—trying to find any bit of humor to escape the horror of the gruesome scene.

About two hours into the wait for the experts to arrive, a Ford Explorer inched up the driveway and parked.

Cam intercepted Angela's parents, Jim and Teresa Swensen, after they'd exited their car; the sheriff blocked access to the house.

Jim tried to sidestep Cam, while Angela's mother cowered behind her husband like a broken shadow. Cam braced himself, trying to imagine how he'd feel if it were one of his kids behind that door. But he couldn't fathom that level of grief. Couldn't imagine facing that horror.

Jim asked, "Is it true? What Becca saw inside the house?"

Damn gossipmonger. "What did she tell you?" Cam asked evenly.

"Becca said she saw them both. Dead." His wild eyes turned accusatory. "Did the sheriff's office intend to notify us?"

"Not until we'd dealt with some of the preliminary issues."

Cam hadn't expected this grisly situation would be kept under wraps for long, not in a town this size, especially since both Angela and Jeff and their families were well liked within the community.

"Our Angela. She's really in there," Jim half-whispered.

"Yes, sir. I'm sorry."

"She's... dead."

"Yes, sir, she is. I'm sorry."

"We need to see her."

The image of her bullet-riddled body jumped into Cam's head, unbidden. "You can't. It's a crime scene." And no parent should ever witness such an atrocity done to their child.

"Jeff killed her?"

"It appears so."

Jim's eyes hardened. "Did he attack her? Did she fight back?"

"We're waiting for the DCI folks to arrive and help us sort out what happened."

"How long before they get here?"

"No idea. It's why we didn't contact anyone. So why don't you and Teresa head home and we'll be in touch as soon as we know anything," Cam said gently. "There's nothing you can do here."

Jim shook his head and made a break for it.

Cam swore and started to give chase, but Teresa grabbed the back of his coat, holding him in place. Cam's prosthesis was dicey on an uneven crust of snow—one icy misstep and it could pop off completely. And at six foot five, he could do some damage to tiny Teresa if he tried to knock her down.

Sheriff Shortbull had been watching the events unfold and he'd intercepted Jim before the grief-stricken father ducked around the back of the house.

But he hadn't kept Jim from seeing the bloody footprints in the snow that led from the back door to the detached garage and then back inside.

Jim fell to his knees, releasing an agonized wail that ripped Cam's soul. Teresa immediately let go of Cam. He turned, expecting to see her racing toward her anguished husband, but she was making a beeline for the unmanned front door of her daughter's house.

Fuck.

Cam snagged her arm, stopping her, and managed to duck when she took a swing at him.

"Let me go! I have to see her! I have to know that she's really—"

"Trust me when I tell you that you don't want to see her like that. Please. Mrs. Swensen. Listen to me. Don't try to go in there again. It's for the best."

Teresa crumpled to the ground and wept.

He couldn't do a damn thing but stand beside her and listen while she sobbed inconsolably. Wishing he were anyplace else but here, watching a family's life forever changed.

And just when Cam thought it couldn't get any worse, another car barreled up the driveway.

Both Jim and Teresa turned to look with hope on their faces. Almost as if they expected this *death thing* had been a horrible mix-up, and Angela would be climbing out of the car.

Cam squinted. Was that Angela's sister, Monica?

Then snow flew as Jim and Teresa raced toward the Lincoln.

When Sheriff Shortbull yelled, "McKay. Call for backup. Now!" Cam realized the car contained Jeff's parents, Bob and Sharon Wingate.

Jesus. Now they'd have try to preserve the crime scene and prevent four grieving parents from ripping each other apart.

After Cam called in an immediate request for assistance, he hustled over to help the sheriff, who was dodging blows from Jim Swensen as he tried to stop Jim from attacking Bob Wingate.

Screaming and obscenities echoed to Cam's left as Teresa rained down her frustration on Sharon. She punctuated each harsh word with a hard shove, until Sharon lost her footing on the ice and fell on her butt. Then Teresa pounced on her.

Before Cam could separate the hair-pulling pair, Sharon flipped Teresa on her back and pummeled her in the face, knocking her out cold.

Heartsick for these families, but forced to do his job, Cam gently pried Sharon away from Teresa. Then he corralled Bob as the sheriff slapped a pair of handcuffs on Jim. Cam had no choice but to handcuff Bob, too.

No matter how hard he tried, he couldn't tune out the venom Bob spewed at him. At the sheriff. At Jim. When Jim shrieked back, sounding more like a wounded animal than a man, Cam wished he had gags. And earplugs. And a different goddamn job.

Sheriff Shortbull shoved Jim into the back of his patrol car and Cam put Bob in his car. Then they went to deal with the mothers.

Teresa had come around. She blinked, as if waking up from a bad dream. When she saw Sharon, Teresa ignored the blood dripping down the front of her coat and charged her.

Cam and the sheriff ended up cuffing both women and placing them in the cars with their respective husbands.

Before Cam closed the door, Bob's accusation rang out loud and clear. "Why didn't you help him?"

Cam froze. "Excuse me?"

"My boy. Jeff. He came back from war... broken. Not on the outside like you." Bob's pain-filled eyes dropped to Cam's left leg. "But on the inside. That's worse. You knew him. You should've tried... You should've reached out to him."

Cam had no response for that. He just quietly shut the door.

****

Thirty minutes later, Angela's sister showed up and whisked her parents away, promising to keep them under lock and key. Immediately following their departure, Jeff's brother, Cliff, appeared to take custody of Bob and Sharon.

Deputy Rick parked at the end of the road, keeping other curious onlookers at bay. Finally, at two o'clock, the DCI vans arrived.

The sheriff walked the techs through the scene and left the house as quickly as possible.

Neither he nor Cam said anything in the four hours the DCI took to catalogue the scene, bag the victims and tag the evidence.

As near as the DCI experts could figure, the bodies had expired within an hour of each other. No sign that anyone else had been in the house with them. It looked as if Jeff Wingate had pulled out his .22 and emptied all fifteen clips into Angela, right in their bedroom.

Then Jeff had walked through her blood, leaving bloody footprints from the bedroom to the garage, and picked up the—

"Sheriff? Deputy? We're finished."

Cam and Sheriff Shortbull faced the crime scene tech, a petite blonde, early twenties, with a waxy complexion and haunted eyes. She reminded Cam of his daughter Liesl. He couldn't imagine his sweet daughter seeing something this horrific. Would the young lady speak to her parents about the atrocities she saw in her job?

Who do you speak to about the atrocities you've seen?

No one.

"Do you need anything else from us?" the sheriff asked.

"No. My boss will be out to wrap up. I just…" She glanced back at the house and shivered. "I've never seen anything like that."

"Glad to know we're not the only ones," the sheriff said.

Cam wasn't surprised the sheriff tried to put the young woman at ease, but the normally congenial man couldn't even muster a smile.

After another brief conversation, the vans pulled away. No sirens. No flashing lights. No hurry.

Darkness had fallen. Cam wasn't a believer in ghosts. But if any apparitions or memory echoes were to appear, it'd be on a night like this. Pitch black. No moon. Wisps of snow clouds scuttled across the dark sky with wraithlike fingers.

They'd opted not to drape the house—or the access to it—in crime scene tape. Locals knew where Jeff and Angela lived. They'd drive by out of morbid curiosity and disbelief.

News crews from Cheyenne, Casper and Denver would figure out the location—no need to make it easy on them. Guaranteed this case would become newsworthy. Local couple found in a murder/suicide on Valentine's Day. He just hoped some of the details would be kept private. *Details like Jeff's military service? Which you hadn't known about?* He tuned out Bob Wingate's accusation and checked his phone. Six messages from Domini. His wife's escalating concern drove home the point that he couldn't face his family in his present dark mood.

Their brood—six kids adopted over the course of the last three years, ranging in age from two to nine—was loud, messy, fierce, loving, joyful and determined. Going home to the family chaos that defined his life was his favorite part of the day. He knew the scene that would greet him. His youngest son, Markus, would be in meltdown mode before supper. His youngest daughter, Sasha, would be watching *Dora the Explorer* for the umpteenth time. The twins, Dimitri and Oxsana would be fighting over the dog. Anton and Liesl would be talking about their classrooms' Valentine's Day parties after finishing chores.

Cam closed his eyes. Had it only been last night he'd sat at the kitchen table with his oldest son and daughter supervising Valentine preparations? Anton finished his Transformers cards in less than twenty minutes, while Liesl had painstakingly written out every classmate's name in red marker. And she'd added a pink squiggle of glitter glue to each paper heart she'd created. By the time Liesl had finished her valentines, she'd been covered in red marker, glue and glitter. She claimed her tongue hurt from licking envelopes, and he'd slipped her an ice cream bar to soothe the sting.

His wife had smiled at them indulgently as she'd directed the twins' placement of candy hearts atop the pink and white frosted cupcakes.

Such innocence didn't need to be tainted by the black cloud surrounding him. Cam texted Domini not to wait up.

Back in Sundance, he parked his patrol car behind the sheriff's office. Both he and the sheriff wrote their reports while the horror was still fresh in their minds. Then they headed to the Golden Boot bar and attempted to dull those too-sharp edges of shock.

Before they'd finished the first beer, people wanted to know what'd really happened with the Wingates. Some even offered hypothetical motives. As an elected official, the sheriff couldn't be rude. He answered questions with grace and ease that looked completely effortless, but Cam could see it was taking a toll on the man.

Finally, Lettie, the bar owner, spirited them to the back, away from continual interruptions. She dropped off a round and said, "I don't know if this is useful information, but Jeff and Angela were in here three days ago."

"And how did they seem?" the sheriff asked.

"Jeff looked a little rough around the edges. Angela kept fussing at him. Urging him to eat. Touching him."

"Did that irritate him?"

"On the contrary. It appeared to soothe him."

"So they weren't fighting?"

"No. They even danced once before they left. It was sweet. They only ever had eyes for each other as teenagers." She looked at Cam with sad eyes. "Don't you remember they were crowned king and queen of the winter formal in their junior year? We were all so happy they reconnected after Jeff moved back home a few years ago." She clucked her tongue. "Those poor families. Left to wonder why. I don't envy you guys your jobs."

"Me neither," Cam mumbled into his beer.

The sheriff sighed. "There goes the jealous rage theory."

They drank in silence until a shadow fell across the table. Cam looked up as Doctor Joely Monroe, a feisty redhead with gamine features and a brusque manner, scooted next to the sheriff in the booth.

"Hey, Doc," Cam said. "I imagine it's not a coincidence that you're here?" As the only physician in the area, chances were good she'd treated the victims at some point in the last few years.

"I'm meeting some folks later, but I figured I'd find you guys drinking after the day you've had." She lowered her voice. "So it's true? About Jeff and Angela?"

"Afraid so."

"Shit." She sighed and shoved her hand through her hair, making the short red tresses stick straight up. "I don't know if it matters, but Angela was my patient."

"Was Jeff?"

"No." Doctor Monroe motioned Lettie over to the table. "Two lemon drop martinis, each with a lemon vodka chaser." She gestured to them. "You guys want anything?"

Sheriff Shortbull shook his head.

Cam said, "Ah, no. I'm good."

They waited in silence until Lettie returned with the drinks. After the doc upended her first martini, she asked, "Can you tell me what happened?"

"Damndest thing. We're not exactly sure," Sheriff Shortbull said and relayed the events. "Do you know anything that could shed light on this case?"

Her shrewd gaze winged to his. "Who will hear this?"

"I'd like to assure you that it'll stay between us, but these things have a way of getting out. You know that. Especially in this case, because everyone is trying to make sense of… something in this fucked-up situation."

She nodded. Fiddled with the stem of her martini glass. "I can tell you that I recently found out Jeff suffered from PTSD."

Cam's gut clenched for the second time at the reminder he'd had no idea Jeff had served in the military, let alone in a combat unit. As Cam tried to think back to the past few years and whether he'd simply forgotten that piece of information, Bob Wingate's accusations pushed front and center. *You should have reached out to him.*

"Angela came into the office last week for her annual checkup. She had bruises on her arms and legs. When I asked why, she said Jeff had been suffering from more combat nightmares than usual. He thrashed around a lot at night and she bore the brunt of it."

Cam felt himself nodding. Those types of flashbacks were so real he woke covered in sweat, his throat raw from heat and sand, feeling like he'd been in the desert fighting for his life.

"Was Angela concerned for her safety?" the sheriff asked.

Doc Monroe shook her head. "She swore she knew how to handle it. Handle him. I had no reason not to believe her or I would've suggested she stay someplace safer." She drained the vodka shot. "I see abused women in my practice far too often. I never would've put Angela in that category."

"Can you back up?" Cam said. "Bob Wingate said something to me earlier, and you just confirmed it, but I had no idea Jeff was a combat vet."

"Me neither," Sheriff Shortbull added. "And I've bowled with Jeff the last few years."

"My understanding is he was a supply clerk in the National Guard. His unit, based out of Laramie, where he joined during college, got called for Operation Iraqi Freedom. They saw the worst of the initial resistance. Jeff was stationed over there about... a year, I guess." Doc Monroe looked at Cam. "You weren't around then."

"Because I was also in Iraq."

"Angela said he wouldn't speak of that time. Like it'd never happened. As soon as he'd fulfilled his enlistment requirements, he moved back to Sundance from Laramie. She knew he'd been diagnosed with PTSD, but his family had no idea. He refused counseling or medication. And ninety-nine percent of the time he was fine."

But that unstable one percent was the unknown—and in this case, a real killer.

Cam ordered another round for himself. Much like Jeff, he didn't talk to his family about being a combat survivor. If he hadn't needed his prosthesis checked twice a year, he'd probably never step foot in the VA. After he'd lost his leg, part of his hand, and received an honorable medical discharge, he'd cut himself off from everyone in his former military life except for a couple guys from his unit.

"I don't mean to be gross, but Jeff really... offed himself with a chainsaw?" Doc Monroe asked.

The sheriff nodded. "The modern day method of falling on his sword. Except he turned it on and..." He drained his beer. "Evidently, it was an older model with no safeguards. It stayed on and kept cutting through everything in its path until it ran out of gas."

Both the sheriff and Cam shuddered at the gruesome mental image of the carnage left in the wake of a runaway chainsaw.

Doc Monroe polished off her second martini. "I'm not a detective, but do any of the pieces fit together yet?"

"More now than they did before you joined us. So thanks, Doc. I'll have to add the supposition to my report."

"The supposition being…" She paused and then said, "That Angela must've startled Jeff during one of his combat nightmares and he emptied his handgun into her. When he realized what he'd done, he killed himself in a manner which he knew he wouldn't survive."

"That's probably as close to the truth as we'll ever get," Cam said. "No one will ever really know what went on."

She looked at them, her brow furrowed, and Cam knew she'd gone back into doctor mode. "But it's not like either of you can easily forget it. Since you have access to a top-notch counselor through the sheriff's office, I recommend you both take advantage of it. This has the potential to haunt you and affect your job."

"Thanks for that cheery reminder," the sheriff said dryly. He grabbed his hat off a peg on the wall. "I'll get someone to drive me home." Once he stood by the end of the booth, he told Cam, "Take tomorrow off. But let me know how you're doin', okay?"

Cam nodded. His cell phone buzzed with a text message, which he ignored.

Doc Monroe signaled someone behind him and finished her last shot. "Will you be all right if I take off too?"

No. "Yeah."

The pushy doc angled across the table, forcing his attention. "I know you, Deputy Cameron McKay. Don't do this to yourself."

"Do what? Wonder why I had no freakin' clue about Jeff's military service? Maybe I could have—"

"You couldn't have done anything. He would've turned away your help if you'd offered."

Probably true. But it didn't diminish his feelings of guilt.

"I can also see you're worried part of you is like Jeff, because you also suffer from PTSD. That one night you'll wake up disoriented and you'll open fire on your family. Cam, that won't ever happen. Not with you."

Pissed him off that she'd picked up on that. "How can you be so sure? No one would've predicted a fucking insurance salesman would fill his wife's body with bullets."

She gave him an intense look. "What do you do with your gun when you're done with your shift?"

He frowned at her. "Either leave it locked up at work or lock it in the gun safe at home."

"Do you have any unattended firearms anywhere in your house right now?"

"No."

"Are any of the firearms in your house loaded? Even the ones locked in the gun safe?"

"Nope."

"Where is your gun safe?"

"In the garage."

"So if you happened to wake up disoriented from a combat nightmare, you couldn't just reach for your gun beneath your pillow or pull it from the nightstand drawer. You'd have to grab your crutches, hobble from your bedroom to the garage, use the keys to open the gun safe, pick a firearm, and load the right clip into the gun itself. Now you're ready to aim and fire, correct?"

"Yeah."

"Think you'd still be asleep after all that? Think you wouldn't have a conscious thought about what you were doing?"

"No, but I have woken up with my goddamn hands wrapped around Domini's neck," he snapped. "Do you have any idea how much that eats at me?" He held out his shaking hands. "Look at these paws. One swipe, one unconscious twist, and I could hurt her. I could even kill her. Just like—"

"No. No. No. No. No." She punctuated every *no* with a loud smack on the table. "You aren't like Jeff Wingate. Not at all. Not even fucking close, Cam. He never faced his demons. You are fully aware of yours. That at least gives you a fighting chance at knowing how to chase them away."

Cam almost said something flip about facing his six demon kids everyday, but he held back.

"I know you have a million McKay family members, but somehow I don't think you let them see this conflicted side. Except for maybe... Keely?"

"I used to. But..." It felt like he was betraying Domini even talking to his sister about such intensely emotional baggage. Yet, he didn't want to talk to his wife about it, either.

Maybe if you don't talk to someone about this shit you will *end up just like Jeff Wingate.*

"If you want a fresh pair of ears, Cam, I'm around. Completely confidential. Anytime."

"I appreciate it, Doc. Thanks."

She patted his hand. "You're welcome. Now I have to scoot and meet my Valentine's Day dates."

"Dates? As in more than one?" Cam asked to her retreating back. He poked his head around the edge of the booth and watched his cousins, Chet and Remy West, escorting the lovely and lively doc from the bar.

Huh. Maybe he was drunker than he thought.

But that didn't keep Cam from drinking steadily over the next couple hours. Everyone left him alone, left him mired in thoughts ranging from morose to manic to plain moronic.

So he was shocked when his brother Colt slid into the booth opposite him. "Am I hallucinating? My recovering alcoholic big bro is in... a bar?"

"Yep. I am here to haul your drunken ass home."

"Who called you?" That'd come out belligerent.

"Lettie called Domini. Domini called me. She knows I won't be tempted to linger in here with you and suck down what's left of the keg." Colt squinted at the empty pitcher of beer and then at Cam. "And I'm strong enough to carry you into the house if need be. Will I hafta do that, Deputy Bro?"

"Probably if I have any more. But I've been done drinking for a while."

"Good." Colt motioned and Lettie appeared. "Can we leave out the kitchen door?"

"Just like old times, huh?" Lettie snickered. "Sneakin' two McKay boys out the back."

Cam's wobbliness had nothing to do with his bum leg and Colt propped him up without Cam having to ask.

On the ride home, Colt said, "So from what I've heard, a bad day on the job?"

"The worst." He thought back to the night his cousin Luke had died. "One of the worst, for sure."

"Domini's beside herself with worry. Especially after she found out you were first on the scene this morning. And then she hasn't heard a word from you except a single text."

This day was a clusterfuck from one end to the other. "I just... I didn't feel like talking about it. I still don't."

"Understood."

Cam closed his eyes and leaned back into the headrest. After a bit he said, "I suppose it's too late to quit my job as a deputy and start ranching fulltime?"

Colt snorted. "No dice. You'd last two days and I'd have to pick up your slack. Besides, you're a good cop, Cam. You're doing exactly what you oughta be. Yeah, some days are gonna suck ass. Part of life. Crawling into a bottle ain't the way to deal with it."

"I know."

"You see bad shit on a daily basis that most people don't ever see. Do you have a way to cope with it?"

"Like blathering on to a shrink or something? No."

"You deal with it all yourself?"

"Yep."

Of course that wasn't the end of the discussion. Colt kept pushing. "You're gonna bring the bad stuff from your job home sometimes. Don't try and hide it. Let your kids and your wife see that your working life ain't all roses and bein' treated like a hero. Let them be the light to ward off the darkness that comes with your job."

Few people gave Colt credit for being insightful, but Colt had been through some bad things in his life and his advice was solid. Cam whistled. "Whoa, bro. That's almost poetic."

Colt laughed. "You're drunker than I thought if you're callin' me a poet. Come on. I'll help you inside."

Cam lowered himself to the ground and accepted Colt's help getting up the steps.

Domini met them on the porch. The kids were still up and she shooed Liesl, Anton, Dimitri, Oxsana and their dog, Gracie, back inside. She slipped her arm inside Cam's coat and he welcomed her warmth. Her support. The unconditional love that reminded him he was the luckiest man alive to get to come home to her every night.

She said, "Thank you, Colt, for bringing him home."

"No problem."

Cam pressed his lips on the top of Domini's head. Inhaling her familiar scent. But she didn't let the affectionate gesture linger. She pulled him into the house. Into the chaos that he normally reveled in.

But the lights were too bright. The TV too loud. Gracie barked and whined when Anton scolded her. Liesl chattered like a magpie, purposely talking over the twins.

Colt clapped him on the back. "Whenever I think my house is a zoo with two kids, it's good to come to your place. Makes our house look like a freakin' monastery. Call me if you need anything."

Cam nodded and the door slammed behind his brother.

Domini unbuttoned his coat and removed it. She slid her hands up his chest and wreathed her arms around his neck, pressing her lithe body against his. "I was worried about you. Are you all right?"

No. I'm not even fucking close to all right.

She eased back and peered into his face. "I can see you're not." She rose to her toes, kissed his mouth and whispered, "What can I do?"

"Just let me crawl into bed and put this day behind me."

"Cam, it's Valentine's Day. The kids planned a special surprise for you."

"I-I can't... be around them. I c-can't let them see me like this."

"Just for a little while? They've been waiting."

He shook his head and closed his eyes, not able to bear their disappointed faces. "I can't. Not tonight. I need to be alone."

"Daddy, wait until you see what—"

"Liesl. Honey, remember what we talked about?" Domini said.

"I told you it was a dumb idea," Anton taunted.

"You're a dumb idea," Liesl retorted.

Anton and Liesl argued.

Then Oxsana and Dimitri argued.

Markus beat on a xylophone and Sasha yelled at him to stop until he began to cry.

The phone started to ring.

The dog yipped.

Cam walked down the hallway to their bedroom and shut the door.

Alone in the silence. He could hear himself breathing in the blessed quiet.

Then gruesome images and coulda-woulda-shoulda regrets pushed this day's awful events into the flashes of death from his military past, so it was like a horror movie stuck on replay—a speeded-up version of a movie that he couldn't get to shut off even if he closed his damn eyes.

Why had he thought he'd wanted to be alone? His mind wasn't a quiet void. In fact, it was a damn unpleasant place to be today.

He stripped and removed his prosthesis. Grabbing his crutches, he headed for the shower. He remained under the steaming spray until his fingers were pruny and he'd run out of tears.

Five minutes after he crawled between the sheets and lay there in the darkness, staring at the ceiling, he heard Domini enter their bedroom and lock the door. Then her warm, naked body slid next to his. Her cool hands caressed his face.

He sighed. This woman filled his life with more happiness than he'd ever known. She deserved better than a man who retreated when his dark edges emerged. But better to be a ghost of a man who disappeared rather than a monster of a man who pointed a gun at her and pulled the trigger.

"The kids are in bed."

"I'm sorry I didn't help with them tonight. I know they—"

"Cam. Baby. It's okay. Tomorrow is a new day."

He squeezed his eyes shut against a rush of tears. He turned his head and kissed the inside of her wrist. "I love you."

"I know you do. I also know you probably don't want to talk about what happened." Her fingers ruffled the hair on his chest. "Even though your body is still, I can tell you're restless."

His cock was starting to stir with her every teasing caress over his skin. Definitely not suffering from whiskey dick.

"Let me help you with that restlessness, Cam." Her fist closed around his thickening shaft. "Just relax and let me ease you."

His whole body seized up. Ease him? Like she was doing him a goddamned favor? He half-snarled, "Is this a pity fuck?" before he could bite it back.

But his sexy wife emitted a throaty laugh and lightly slapped his dick. "Yes, because it's such a chore to put my hands all over your strong body. It's pure torture. I don't know how I'll ever bear it." She nipped his shoulder with her teeth. "But somehow, I'll suffer through and take one for team McKay."

He smiled for the first time in what seemed like days. "Such a noble sacrifice."

"I figured you'd appreciate it." She angled forward to lick his nipple. Goose flesh rippled down his abdomen. "Besides. It *is* Valentine's Day and I'll get cranky if I don't get laid." She pressed kisses from the tip of his chin up his jawline to his ear. "Very, very cranky, since I'm pretty sure you didn't get me a gift."

"Dom, I don't know—"

"Don't tell me you're not up for this." She squeezed his erection. "Because I'm holding the ultimate lie detector and it's saying... mount up."

Cam groaned and rolled his hips into her stroking hand.

"You need a reminder of what's good and a chance to forget the bad. Since the word *ease* pushed your buttons, how about this... Sir, will you let me have my wicked way with you?"

A bold move on Domini's part, asking for control. Outside the bedroom they were equal partners in all things. But here, in their private space, with the door locked, Domini surrendered her sexual will to him. Completely. Without question.

"Say the word to me, Cam, so I don't give you a reason to bend me over your knee and paddle my butt for insubordination."

He twisted his fingers around the chain dangling from her neck, a symbol of the bond between them few would understand. She always knew exactly what he needed. He tugged her closer by the chain and murmured, "Yes. Make me forget."

Domini kissed him with teasing sweetness that gradually heated into passion. She pinned his arms above his head and used every sexual trick in her repertoire to drive him wild. To blank his mind to everything but his frenzied need for her.

Then she connected their bodies and began to move on him. Taking her time, so he felt every sensuous glide of her soft skin over the rougher rasp of his. Whispering Ukrainian endearments in his ear. Each slide of their sweat-coated bodies drove them higher until finally they tumbled over the edge into that vortex of pleasure together.

Although winded—and sated—Cam wasn't ready to return to reality. Didn't want ugliness to intrude on the beautiful gift of peace Domini had given him. He wanted to stay in this cocoon for a little while longer. He rolled Domini to her back and whispered, "Again," losing himself in her heat and softness and goodness.

Then he slept in her arms, in a surprisingly dreamless sleep.

****

The next morning Domini poked him to get up—way, way too early since he didn't have to work and the kids were out of school.

Cam rolled over, pulling the pillow over his head, intending to sleep the day away.

He should've known better than to try and thwart his wife, the woman who regularly got six kids up and ready for the day. She opened their bedroom door and let the dog in. An open door was an open invitation, and soon Markus and Sasha climbed onto the bed, crawling all over him. Offering hugs, kisses and giggles as their wiggly bodies began to bounce on the mattress. Then the twins joined in the fun, laughing hysterically at their live game of *Hop on Pop,* which happened to be a favorite family book. Then Anton joined the fray. Showing off karate kicks and spins.

Cam grinned at his exuberant kiddos, having so much fun with the forbidden activity. If he still had both legs he probably would've joined them. So he egged them on.

A gasp. Then, "Cameron West McKay! You're letting them jump on the bed?"

"Yep." And wasn't his wife a good little actress? Pretending to be indignant when she'd known that he needed to be surrounded by all their smiling faces first thing this morning.

"Off," she said, pointing to each kid in turn.

"But, Mom—"

"Sorry, kids. Mommy is right. No more monkeys jumping on the bed."

They reluctantly bounced off and raced out of the room, laughing.

Speaking of laughing… Where was Liesl? She was always in the thick of things. But since she, too, wore a pirate's leg—the phrase she used to describe her prosthesis—she'd probably seen no point in trying to do a one-legged hop.

He dressed, using his crutches, not bothered in the least that his stump hung out. It'd taken a while for him to feel comfortable letting his family see that broken part of him.

He came back from the war… broken… on the inside. Why didn't you reach out to him?

Dammit. He was not going there today. He was *not* Jeff Wingate.

Cam swung into the kitchen as saw Liesl sitting alone at the breakfast bar. She beamed a sunny smile his way as soon as she saw him. "Daddy!"

"Mornin', punkin'."

Liesl crawled onto his lap immediately after he sat down. She hugged him tightly and sighed heavily. Then her gap-toothed smile faded.

"Something wrong?"

"Mommy said you were too tired last night for my Valentine's Day surprise."

"Yes, I was. Sorry, sweetheart. Sometimes my job makes me tired."

"Does it make you sad? 'Cause you looked kinda sad last night."

Cam tucked a flyaway strand of blond hair behind Liesl's ear. "Yeah, I was sad, too."

"Why?"

He struggled to put it in terms she could understand without putting a rainbows-and-butterflies spin on it. "Because I saw a bad thing."

His normally animated daughter wore a somber look. "I was scared."

"Scared of what?"

"Scared that someone hurted you and that's why you were so sad."

"Oh, no, Liesl, honey. I'm sorry you were scared. No one hurt me. Doing my job… sometimes I see stuff that hurts me inside."

She nodded and her pigtails bounced. "Sometimes, when I'm sad, my heart hurts." Then she bent forward and placed a kiss on his chest. "Did that make it feel better?"

Tears sprang to Cam's eyes. He pulled his precious girl closer to the heart she owned. "Yes, sweetheart, it really did."

Liesl squirmed away. "Now can I give you the surprise?"

He chuckled at the rapid reminder of her short attention span. "By all means. What is it?"

"First, you gotta wear this." She grabbed a gold paper crown she'd embellished with pink glitter glue swirls and tiny hearts cut from construction paper. "You get to be the King of Hearts."

Cam froze. That was the title given to the king and queen of the junior winter formal. The title that Jeff Wingate had worn.

A happy, humming Liesl tugged the crown over his head, repositioning it until it was exactly how she wanted it. Then she noticed his change in posture. "Daddy, what's wrong? Is the crown too tight?"

"No. It's just…"

She placed her hands on his cheeks and stared into his eyes. "Does your heart hurt again? 'Cause I can give it another kiss. Sometimes, it takes a whole bunch."

And sometimes in a single instant, it just took the sweetness of one little girl, the happy screaming laughter of his kids, and the loving indulgence of his wife to set everything in his world right again.

That's when he really understood he was nothing like Jeff Wingate. When the darkness encroached, he didn't hide in it for long. He let his wife and children be the forces of nature that pulled him back into the light where he belonged.

"Are you worried that Mommy might feel bad because you're the king? Because every king needs a queen, Daddy, *everyone* knows that. So Mommy has a crown, too. She's the Queen of Hearts. I put purple hearts on yours because Mommy said a purple heart is a sign of bravery."

"What color are the hearts on Mommy's crown?"

"Red. Because red means love."

"Yes, indeed it does. Mommy is all full of love, isn't she?" He cleared his throat. "So are you. Making us matching crowns is a good surprise, Liesl. Thank you."

Liesl snorted. "Daddy, that's *not* the surprise."

"It's not? There's more?"

"Yes!" She clapped her hands. "We're gonna put on a Valentine's Day play for the King and Queen! All of us. Even the little kids. Even Gracie. It's all set up in my bedroom. Everyone is waiting for me to bring the king so the show can start."

His theatrical daughter loved to put on a show. That meant impromptu costumes and props from the barn and cardboard backdrops done in crayon, and live music—usually kazoos, a xylophone, maracas, drums and a harmonica—basically full out chaos, kids fighting and screaming and crying, popcorn on the carpet and spilled juice. A total mess that'd take three days to clean up.

He couldn't wait to be a part of it.

Cam adjusted his crown, smiled at his daughter, and bowed formally, while holding onto his crutches. "Well, then, Princess Liesl, lead the way."

She giggled. "Daddy, You're silly."

"That's your highness to you, young lady. Come on. The King of Hearts can't keep his subjects waiting, can he?"

ROUGH ROAD

A Rough Riders novella featuring Chassie, Trevor, and Edgard from *Rough, Raw, and Ready.*

AUTHOR'S NOTE

This story runs concurrently with the first chapters of Rough Riders book 14— *Gone Country*...

CHAPTER ONE

"Mama, what's a faggot?"

Chassie's entire body seized up and she nearly dropped the bowl she was washing. She turned her head and met the startled eyes of her husband Trevor, who was packaging leftovers on the counter beside her. She managed to ask, "Where'd you hear that word?" in a steady voice.

"At school. A third-grader said my dads were faggots."

She briefly closed her eyes. Living an unconventional lifestyle in a conservative rural area guaranteed this question would come up at some point—but she hadn't expected it this soon. Their six-year-old son Westin had just started first grade a month ago.

Chassie rinsed and dried her hands before she turned around. "How about if we wait to talk about it until *Papai* is done giving Max his bath? You can stay up a little later tonight."

Westin's big blue eyes were somber, suspicious of the bribe. But he nodded and returned to his "homework"—an activity book they'd purchased after his disappointment at not having schoolwork every night in first grade.

Trevor came over and set his hands on her shoulders. He kissed her temple and whispered, "Come on, Chass. Baby, take a deep breath. We'll get through this. That word doesn't have the power to destroy what we've built unless we let it."

She nuzzled his jaw. "I know that. It's just..."

"Mama!" A little person slammed into the backs of her legs. She glanced down. A naked little person.

Two-year-old Max grinned at her, his brown eyes triumphant, his dark hair sopping wet.

Edgard sauntered into the kitchen, a bath towel draped over his forearm. "That boy is as slippery as an eel." He wrapped the towel around Max like a straightjacket and hoisted him up amidst Max's happy shrieks and giggles. "Kiss Mama and Daddy goodnight, little streaker. Then if we can wrassle your jammies on fast, we'll have time for one book."

"Two books!"

Chassie smooched both of Max's chubby cheeks and smoothed her hand over his wet hair. "'Night, Max. Love you."

Trevor kissed Max's forehead. "Love you son, 'night."

Edgard's gaze winged between Chassie and Trevor. He mouthed, "Problem?"

"I'll fill you in upstairs. I need to check on Sophia anyway," Trevor said. He looked at Chassie. "I'll tuck her in if she hasn't already crashed."

Four-year-old Sophia ran at such high speed all day that many nights she conked out while watching TV or playing in her room.

The guys disappeared upstairs.

Chassie finished cleaning the kitchen and headed to the basement to throw a load of clothes in the washer. Her mind had locked on Westin's question. She knew one thing about her thoughtful son—the taunt hadn't been tossed at him just today. Westin tried to figure things out on his own, so she worried he'd been dealing with defining the nasty word for longer than a day.

She leaned against the wall, fighting tears, fighting memories of the cruelty directed at her growing up. The jeers—lazy Indian, ugly squaw—still lingered years later. Back then she'd been so shy she hadn't fought back. Her brother Dag might've gone after her tormentors, but he'd been fighting his own demons. No doubt he'd had the word faggot hurled at him.

What really caused that long ago hurt to deepen was the knowledge that if their father had known Dag's sexual orientation, he would've flung that word at his son without hesitation.

When Chassie, Edgard and Trevor decided to add kids to their family, they all three worked every day to make sure their children knew they were loved. To make sure their children knew their parents loved each other. And to show them that love is what built and what sustained their lives. Especially when it was love that a lot of people didn't understand.

Chassie held on to that thought as she scaled the stairs.

Westin spun around in his chair and looked at her.

She smiled. "How about a cup of hot chocolate while we're waiting for Daddy and *Papai?* And I can check over your homework."

****

Trevor found a pajama-clad Sophia asleep, stretched out on the floor, coloring books, crayons and chalk scattered around her. The girl burned with jealousy that Westin went to school all day, so she'd started her own school. Since her little brother, Max, was too young to sit still for longer than three minutes, she'd lined up her dolls and stuffed animals as students. She'd crafted individual desks out of boxes and set up her classroom. Such a creative, whimsical girl.

Trevor returned the crayons to the box and set her teaching supplies on her desk next to the pink plastic tea set. Then he scooped her into his arms and stepped around the debris strewn across the floor.

Sophie stirred briefly.

"Hey, sweetheart. It's bedtime."

"But, Daddy, I'm not tired."

Trevor grinned. Much like her mother, the girl fought sleep, regardless if she was already asleep. "In you go." Trevor laid her on the unmade bed. He pulled off her socks and tucked the purple satin covers around her.

She gave him a sleepy smile and reached her arms up for a hug.

He closed his eyes and just held on to her, this sweet child who filled all their lives with so much joy. He nestled her head in the pillow and kissed her cheek. "That one is from Mama." He kissed her other cheek. "That one is from *Papai*." He kissed her forehead. "And that one is from me." He brushed her long, dark hair over her shoulder. "Want the night light on?"

"Uh-huh." Her gaze darted to the floor. "Can you get Mr. Tuttles? He's scared to sleep on the floor."

"Of course." He still thought it a strange name for her favorite bear, but she'd chosen it out of the blue at age two and it'd stuck. He snagged the panda and tucked it next to her. "'Night, darlin' girl. Love you."

"Love you too, Daddy."

Trevor plugged in the nightlight and left the door open a crack before he headed down the hallway to the master bedroom.

He removed his long-sleeved shirt and T-shirt, tossing them in the hamper along with his dirty jeans. After washing his face and arms, he slipped on a pair of black sweatpants and a gray tank top. He'd need to channel his frustration after they talked to Westin, because guaranteed he'd wanna punch the shit out of something.

Faggots. Who taunted a kid—a kind, innocent little boy—with that term?

You would have.

Goddamn. Trevor didn't want to think along those lines, to remember the judgmental asshole he'd been at one time. He'd been raised that way—as had Chassie and Edgard—which was why they were raising their kids differently.

He perched on the edge of their gigantic custom-made bed, forearms resting on his thighs, his face aimed at the carpet. Westin and Sophia were aware their family was different from the norm. But due to divorces and remarriages, didn't most kids these days deal with multiple parents? How was it anyone's business how they lived in their own home? Or how they loved each other? He'd bet the ranch very few traditional family units were as attuned to each other as theirs. They *had* to work harder at communication because of having a third partner. And he wouldn't have it any other way—regardless of the societal repercussions.

Footsteps fell across the carpet. A pause. "Did you mean to leave the light on in Sophia's room?" Edgard asked.

"No. Guess my mind was elsewhere." Trevor glanced up. "Was she still awake?"

"Nah. She just yanked the covers over her head. I shut the light off."

"Thanks. And Max?"

"Out. He didn't last through one book, let alone two." Edgard gave Trevor a once-over. "We working out tonight?"

"I'll need to hit the heavy bag after..."

"After what?"

He sighed.

"Trev, what's goin' on?"

So Trevor told him.

Edgard didn't say anything. Then he crouched in front of Trevor to get his attention. "That's not all of what's bugging you."

The man knew him so well. Trevor reached out and ran the back of his knuckles along Edgard's jaw. He hadn't shaved for a day and Trevor had the sudden need to feel beard burn on the inside of his thighs. On his chest. Scraping on his cheeks and neck as he kissed Edgard senseless.

"Dangerous to keep lookin' at me like that, *meu amor*. Burning me alive with those fiery eyes of yours won't make me forget the issue at hand, as much as I'd like to."

"I know." Trevor dropped his hand. "I fuckin' hate that I used to be that type of kid Westin is dealin' with. Anything I didn't understand, I belittled. I laughed when I made kids cry. *Laughed*. Jesus. How many people I bullied growing up would say I'm getting what I deserve? Seeing *my* son cry." He exhaled. "I'm to the point I can handle what anyone calls us. But it breaks my damn heart that Westin is hearing that shit."

"Hey. You're not the same man you were. Thank God for that." Edgard stood and held his hand out to Trevor. "Worrying about karma coming back to bite you in the ass won't help us now."

As soon as he was upright, Trevor tugged Edgard against his body and buried his face in Edgard's neck. "I'm grateful every damn day that we have this life."

"Me too. We knew goin' into it, it wouldn't be easy."

"Some days I can't believe we've all been together eight years. And other days, I feel like my life started when I met Chassie and you came back." Trevor lifted his head. "Do you think we oughta cancel—"

Edgard covered his mouth with a brief kiss. "No. The three of us need the time together. Chassie will be relieved that we'd planned to keep Westin out of school tomorrow anyway."

"So we're all set?"

"Yep."

Trevor grinned. "Chass is really gonna be surprised."

"I was surprised. It was a sweet, romantic thing to plan, Trev."

"What can I say? You and Chassie bring out the best in me." Trevor kissed him, more than a soft peck but less than the tongue tangling soul kiss he preferred. "Let's go talk to our son."

****

Edgard kept his hands on Trevor's shoulders as they returned to the kitchen.

Chassie sat at the head of the table with Westin on her lap. He poked the marshmallows in his cup of hot chocolate.

They each took a seat beside Chassie.

"So I checked Westin's workbook and he got one hundred percent." She brushed his blond hair from his forehead. "Our smart boy also translated five words into Portuguese."

Edgard said, "I'm proud of you," in Portuguese, which brought Westin's quick smile. Chassie and Trevor were learning the language, just not as fast as the kids.

"Maybe *Papai* oughta get me'n Mama a Portuguese workbook, so we don't fall behind you and your sister."

"I'd help you with it, Daddy. You too, Mama," Westin added.

"I know you would, son. You're a helpful, thoughtful boy."

Everyone fell quiet.

"So someone said something to you at school today?" Edgard asked.

Westin looked up. His gaze winged between Trevor and Edgard. "He said you were faggots."

Edgard's stomach churned. "And you don't know what that word means?"

"Huh-uh. But he said it like it was a bad word. Is it?"

That was truly the vilest F word—in Edgard's opinion.

"It's an ugly word that people who don't understand love say to hurt someone's feelings, and make them feel bad about who they love," Trevor said softly.

Edgard covered Trevor's restless hand with his and threaded their fingers together.

Chassie kissed the top of Westin's head. "See how Daddy and *Papai* are holding hands? They love each other. Some people think that's wrong. That two men shouldn't love each other like that."

"But why not?"

"We honestly don't know."

Trevor and Edgard reached for Chassie's hands at the same time.

"And some people don't think it's right that your Daddy and I love each other, and we both love your mama, and she loves us both back," Edgard said.

Westin silently poked his marshmallows again, his brow furrowed.

Edgard had no idea if any of this was making sense to him. Westin had three loving parents. He was used to seeing *Papai* kissing Mama and Daddy. It was normal for Westin and his siblings to witness the love and affection that all three of his parents had for each other. In what universe was that wrong?

"You're kinda quiet. Do you have any questions?"

Westin shook his head. His blond hair fell across his forehead and Chassie lovingly smoothed it back.

"You sure?" Trevor prompted.

Those blue eyes were enormous when he asked, "He said I'm probably a faggot too. Am I?"

Chassie bit her lip and closed her eyes.

Old memories Edgard thought he'd buried long ago pushed to the surface. The taunts, jeers and accusations that'd been hurled at him since he'd turned thirteen. But Westin was so young, too young to understand why some kid he didn't know felt entitled to say shit like that to him.

Trevor scooted closer and took Westin's hand. "Can I tell you a secret? I used to be one of them mean kids who said words like that, mostly because I didn't know what it meant. I said that kinda stuff because everyone else did. I'm ashamed of that now. It was wrong; it *is* wrong. Faggot, fag, homo—are all awful words that try to make love that's special sound wrong. Do I know if you'll fall in love with a boy or a girl when you're older? Nope. But no matter who you fall in love with son, your love, the way you feel, won't be wrong. And no one has the right to call you names for it."

A lump formed in Edgard's throat. There'd been a time he never would've believed that Trevor Glanzer was capable of feeling that way, let alone admitting it out loud.

"Mama, I'm tired."

"I know you are. Give Daddy and *Papai* a hug and a kiss. Then I'll tuck you in."

"That's okay, Chass. I'll do it," Trevor said and stood.

Westin clung to Chassie for a minute before he crawled off her lap and threw himself at Edgard. He squeezed the boy tightly and kissed the top of his head. "Love you, son. I'm glad you talked to us about this. You can talk to us about anything, you know that, right?"

"Yes, *Papai*."

He released the boy and Trevor scooped him up.

As soon as they left the kitchen, Chassie's tear-filled eyes met his. "How can we...?"

Edgard lifted her onto his lap and cradled her to his chest. "I've got you. Cry if you want."

"I hate to cry."

"I know you do," he soothed. He held her, resting his chin on top of her head, knowing once her frustration ebbed, Mama Bear Chassie would roar.

Chassie stayed quiet, her breath hard and fast.

"What're you thinking about?" he asked after a bit.

"Dag. Havin' to hide who he was. And you. Accepting who you were but havin' to hide it to be with Trevor. And Trevor. Lying to himself about bein' in love with a man. And me. Feeling smug because I have two men who love me. We decided to live the life we want, screw what anyone else thinks, right? Then I worry it's unfair to our kids because they'll have to deal with people around here who think we're freaks. We—you, me and Trev—we're somewhat isolated from those attitudes out here on the ranch. But Westin and Sophia and Max will have to face those attitudes every day when they go to school. I hate that this is just the start." She sighed heavily against his chest. "Homeschooling them—"

"Is an option," Edgard inserted, "but it isn't something we need to worry about now. We answered Westin's question. We reiterated that love between two men isn't wrong, and neither is the love the three of us share. Most kids are lucky if they've got one good parent. Our kids have three *great* parents. They'll grow up happy, Chass, because we won't let them be any other way."

"You're right. It just stings when those crap attitudes hit us in the face through our sweet son." She kissed the side of his throat. "I love you. Thanks for talkin' me down and keeping me from crying. Lord. I've been weepy lately."

Edgard tipped her chin up and looked into her eyes. "Is there some-thing else—"

"I don't know about you," Trevor said as he entered the kitchen, "but I feel like beating the fuck outta my heavy bag."

"Westin have any more questions for you?"

He shook his head. "He sacked right out." He looked at Edgard. "So whatdya say, partner? Wanna go a few rounds?"

As much as Edgard like sparring with Trevor, he wasn't feeling up to it tonight. And he didn't want to leave Chassie alone. "Go ahead. I'll get our woman tucked in and make sure she gets the rest she needs."

Trevor's eyes met his in understanding. "Good. I'll be up in a bit." He ducked down the stairs leading to the basement.

Chassie stood. "I need to shower first. So it's okay if you wanna go pound on Trev."

He waggled his eyebrows. "As much as I like pounding on him, maybe I'd rather scrub your back. I'm feeling a little dirty myself."

"So what else is new?" They held hands as they climbed the stairs.

Their water games were mostly innocent. Edgard kneaded her tensed muscles. His relaxation techniques included caresses and soft kisses. He loved touching her, this woman who defined strength and softness. The depth of his feelings for her at the beginning of their relationship as a triad had surprised him. As did how easily and quickly they brought something to each other besides their love for Trevor.

She squinted at him. "You're looking at me funny, Ed."

"Just thinking about how much I love you."

"You tryin' to get me to cry?"

"No, *querida*, I'm trying to get you to smile. 'Cause I know how much you love bein' reminded that me and Trev are wrapped around your little finger."

Chassie grinned. "It *is* good to be me."

After drying off and slipping on her pajamas, Chassie went to check on the kids one last time, like she always did, even if both he and Trevor had already checked them.

Then she crawled in bed and curled into him, like she did most nights. It'd never bothered him that she'd fall asleep in his arms and wake up in Trevor's arms since Trevor had to have a hand someplace on Edgard's body every night. A constant reassurance that he was really there.

Edgard started to drift off. He heard the shower kick on. Then the familiar scent of soap wafted out on a humid wave as Trevor exited the bathroom. The dresser drawer squeaked and he looked over to see Trevor slipping on a pair of flannel pants. Their days of sleeping in the nude had ended with three kids popping into their room any hour of the night.

So Edgard was really looking forward to the next three days and nights.

Trevor tucked his body behind Chassie's. He reached for Edgard, threading their fingers together and resting their joined hands on the pillow above Chassie's head.

All was right with his world and he let sleep overtake him.

CHAPTER TWO

The next morning Chassie had finished packing Westin's lunch when Edgard wandered into the kitchen. He gave her the brilliant, sexy grin that still weakened her knees. "Mornin', beautiful."

"Mornin' yourself, sleepyhead. Why aren't you helping Trev with the feeding?"

"He said he had it handled." Edgard poured himself a cup of coffee.

Chassie glanced at the clock. "Why aren't the kids up? Westin is gonna miss the bus if we don't leave in ten minutes."

"He says he's got a stomachache and he's not goin' to school today."

Her gut clenched. "Because of what was said to him at school yesterday?"

"No." Edgard curled his hand around her face and pressed a gentle kiss on her lips. "He did have a pained look, so I tucked him back in bed. Didn't see a reason to wake the other kids up."

"I should go check on him."

"Chass. Baby, I just did." He kissed her again and stepped back to sip his coffee. "Did you deal with the goats this morning?"

"Yep." She refilled her coffee cup and looked around the kitchen. Seemed weird the kids weren't up. Mornings were chaotic, but also her favorite part of the day. "I think..." She heard a noise and leaned over to look out the window. A car she didn't recognize had started up the driveway. "Who on earth is dropping by at seven-thirty in the morning?"

The car parked next to the mini-van and a beautiful brunette stepped out. Her hair and makeup perfect; her clothing stylish and unwrinkled. "Omigod. What is my cousin Ramona West doin' here?"

Without waiting for Edgard to respond, Chassie raced out of the house.

Ravishing Ramona paused at the edge of the walkway leading to the front door. She grinned and threw open her arms. "Look at what the cat dragged in all the way from Seattle!"

Chassie hugged her. "You look fantastic, as usual."

"So do you. I see your men are taking great care of you."

"Always. So you could've warned me you were comin' for a visit."

"Nope, that would've ruined the surprise."

"What surprise?"

The front door to the house opened, disgorging all three of their kids, who were jumping on Ramona like eager puppies. Chassie's eyes narrowed at Westin. "Someone wanna tell me what's goin' on?"

Max was running around yelling, "Surprise, Mama, surprise!"

"What surprise?" she repeated.

Trevor's hands were on her shoulders and Edgard flanked her. "The surprise that Ramona is here to stay with the kids for the weekend while we whisk you off to celebrate our anniversary."

Westin grinned. "Had you fooled, huh Mama? You thought I was really sick."

She ruffled his hair, happy to see him smiling after last night's conversation. "Yes. So you were all in on this?"

"Uh-huh." Sophie giggled. "I'm a good secret keeper."

"That you are." Chassie looked over and saw Edgard's truck backed up to the side door and luggage piled in the back. "How long have you two had this planned?"

"About a month," Edgard said. "We asked Keely if she'd take the kids for a weekend, and she mentioned it to Ramona, who had planned to be in Wyoming next week anyway. So she volunteered to come early."

Ramona leaned over and whispered, "Three days of nonstop loud sex with these two hotties who worship you? I'm more than a little jealous, cuz." She scooped Max up and perched him on her hip. "I see the 'why would a single woman volunteer' question in your eyes and the truth is, I fear my brothers will never get married and give me nephews and nieces, so I'm co-opting the Glanzer kids as mine."

Trevor grinned. "Works for us since my family has disowned me and Ed's family is in Brazil. Oh, right, they disowned him too."

"People are stupid. Family is family. I hardly ever get to see Nick and Holly's kids, or Blake and Willow's boys. Boone is all grown up now—I can't believe he's a senior in high school. And our McKay cousins...they've already got ten million aunts and uncles. So the price of my child care duties is this: I expect to be called Aunt Ramona from here on out."

"Yes, Aunt Ramona," Westin said.

"But we already call Keely Aunt Keely," Sophia added. "And India Aunt India—"

"Forget I asked to be special."

"You are special," Westin insisted.

"And you are the sweetest boy in the world." Ramona kissed his cheek. "We are gonna have some fun this weekend."

"So are we."

Edgard aimed Chassie a hot look that made her belly swoop. "You've got five minutes to get your toiletries packed and say goodbye to the kids before we hit the road." He shook his head when Chassie opened her mouth. "And don't ask where we're goin'."

"Just be ready," Trevor added and lightly smacked her ass.

"But who's taking care of the livestock?"

"Colt," Edgard and Trevor said simultaneously. "We've got it handled. You're wasting time, woman."

"Fine." Chassie raced inside and tossed her bathroom stuff in a bag. What had the guys packed for her? Should she check to see they'd packed enough?

Don't worry about it. Chances are high you'll be nekkid most the weekend anyway.

And she couldn't wait.

****

Six hours later they'd reached their destination—a remote cabin in Montana.

Trevor hoisted the last cooler out of the pickup bed. He and Edgard had decided it'd be easiest to haul food with them, rather than trying to find a grocery store in the middle of nowhere. The last thing he wanted to do on this rare getaway was spend time buying groceries.

Inside the cabin, Edgard was putting the food away. He glanced over his shoulder at Trevor and grinned. "This is a great place. Where'd you find it?"

"A couple guys I knew came up here huntin' every fall. Lucky for us this is this weekend before the season opens. Where's Chass?"

"In the bedroom, checking to see what we packed for her."

"That oughta take her all of two minutes." Trevor cut through the large living area to the hallway leading to the bedrooms. The master suite had a king-sized bed and a sitting area. He gave the windows that overlooked a small meadow a cursory glance before tracking Chassie to the master bath. The walk-in slate shower was enormous—perfect for three.

Trevor leaned in the doorframe, watching Chassie paw through the toy bag. Without looking up, she said, "Will we really need three vibrators this weekend?"

"Guess we'll have to wait and see. Better to have too many than too few. And you, my sweet, darlin' wife, have too many clothes on. Strip."

Chassie rolled her eyes and then she brushed past him, setting the bag of sex toys on the floor.

Trevor followed her, stopping at the end of the bed.

Edgard moved in behind him, resting his chin on Trevor's shoulder. "You heard him. Ditch the clothes."

She whirled around. "But we've only been here fifteen minutes."

"Then we've already wasted five of those minutes." Trevor's heart thumped when Edgard's hand splayed across his lower belly. "This retreat is to celebrate ten years of marriage and eight years of our commitment to Ed. Now we're a family, but I wanted us to reaffirm to each other what we are to each other."

"There's more to what the three of us are to each other than awesome sex partners," Chassie shot back.

"But sex is part of who we are, and sometimes that connection gets lost in ranch chores, raising kids and other day-to-day stuff," Edgard said. "And I, for one, am very curious as to what our Trevor has planned for us."

Chassie smirked. "Me too. No doubt Mr. Bossy will tell us in explicit detail."

Trevor raised an eyebrow. "I believe Mr. Bossy already told you to strip."

"Maybe you oughta disobey him," Edgard drawled, "'cause I surely would like to see some red marks across your ass. Been a while, hasn't it?"

"That's a great idea, Ed. Did you pack a crop?"

"Yep."

"That's a terrible idea," Cassie grumbled. "I'm stripping, see?" She whipped her sweatshirt off, then her tank top. Trevor loved that she hadn't worn a bra. She pushed her jeans and plain white panties down her legs, kicking them aside. Naked, she propped her hand on her hip. "Now what?"

"Watch."

Edgard's hand moved and unbuttoned Trevor's jeans. His deft fingers slid the zipper down. One tug and Trevor's jeans and underwear fell to his knees.

Trevor shifted impatiently and kicked them off completely.

Chassie's demeanor changed as she watched them.

Something had changed with Trevor too; his cock was fully erect.

Edgard's hand gripped the base of Trevor's cock and stroked up, adding that twist at the end that had Trevor clenching his butt cheeks together.

"I thought I was in charge," Trevor said.

"You are," Edgard breathed in his ear sending a wave of want through him. "Tell me to stop."

Right. Like that'd happen.

"Didn't think so," Edgard breathed again. "Tell us what you want."

Trevor crooked his finger at Chassie. "On your knees."

She was in front of him in an instant.

"Ed, put my cock in her mouth." Trevor watched as Edgard painted the outline of her lips with the wet tip. Chassie's breath drifted over the sensitive head for a couple of heartbeats. And then his shaft was gliding into her warm, wet mouth, "Sweet Jesus that feels good."

Edgard waited several strokes until Chassie's mouth was wet enough that she could fully take Trevor's shaft. On the next pass, he didn't let her retreat. He held her head in place, her lips pressed against Trevor's groin, his dick filling her throat. "Swallow," Edgard commanded. "You know how he likes it."

Chassie's eyes remained on Trevor's as her throat muscles worked him. And worked him again. And again.

"Beautiful," Trevor murmured and reached down to caress the hollow of her cheek. "You're so perfect in every way. I'm so lucky to have you."

Her eyes fluttered closed and she sighed as she released his cock and started sliding her mouth up and down his shaft.

Then Edgard was unbuttoning Trevor's shirt and tugging it to his elbows. His hands skated across Trevor's torso. Stopping to tease all the hot spots that drove him wild. He hissed with pleasure when Edgard pinched his nipple the same time Chassie's teeth scraped the underside of his cockhead. His lovers knew him well. Knew how to make him shudder and moan. Knew how to make his knees weak and his head spin.

Knew how to make him feel loved.

What they brought to each other like this, stripped down, vulnerable—nothing to hide behind—was love in its purest form.

Warm lips followed the cup of his shoulder to the sweet spot behind his ear. Another pair of warm lips circled the thick tip of his cock. They built a rhythm together and used it without pause to drive him to the brink.

As much as Trevor wanted to close his eyes and lose himself in these erotic sensations, he kept his eyes on his wife. Kept his left hand on her face and his right hand gripped Edgard's hip. Needing to stay connected in the moment. Because any moment he'd fly apart.

"Trev, let go. We've got you," Edgard said against his nape, his heated breath raising gooseflesh.

"Feels too damn good," he said gruffly.

"This is only the appetizer, *meu amor.*" He ground his erection into the cleft of Trevor's ass.

Trevor turned his head and Edgard caught his lips in a flirty kiss. His mind blanked to everything except the hardness of Edgard's body against his and the softness of Chassie's hair wrapped in his fist. The fast, wet, suctioning pulls of her mouth on his dick. The nips and bites on the back of his neck and shoulder. He couldn't hold back any longer.

"Fuck."

He started to come; ass tight, balls tight, teeth gritted. That first blast of heat shot up his dick into Chassie's sucking mouth. She swallowed each burst, her eyes locked to his. On the last spurt, she parted her lips and let his cock slide free, a satisfied smile on her face as she tongued the sensitive tip.

His entire body twitched. "Christ, woman. That was..."

"Trevor speechless. I like that." She pushed to her feet and kissed the tattoo on his left pectoral. "That was fun. What's next?"

"What do you want?"

Her gaze darted to Edgard and then back to him. "I want to watch Ed fuck you."

Trevor wiped come from the corner of her mouth with his thumb. "You do get off on that."

"So do you."

"So do I." Edgard brought Trevor's thumb to his mouth and licked it clean with such long, sensual strokes that Trevor's dick stirred again.

"But that's really what you want?" Trevor prompted Chassie.

"Yep." She stood on tiptoe and kissed him. "Since you brought vibrators, I can get myself off like two or three times while I'm watching." She smirked and tugged off his shirt. "But I do ask that bein's we're not limited to the bedroom since our children aren't around, that you don't come quickly. Or quietly. I wanna hear you. Both of you."

"God, I love you." Trevor wrapped himself around her and kissed with heat and heart, with soul kisses that showed her that she owned him, body and soul.

Edgard retreated and gave them the moment.

When they broke apart, he grinned and pushed her on the bed. "Vibrators are fine. But this first go I'm getting you off with my mouth."

She laughed. "Like I'm gonna argue with that."

Trevor shoved her thighs apart and dove in, growling at the sweet taste of her. "I love that you're so wet after blowing me."

Chassie arched when he jammed his tongue inside her deep. She writhed when he pushed his thumb into her pussy so he could insistently tongue her clit. Little whips, first soft and slow, and then hard and fast. Sucking kisses. Firm-lipped bites.

The way her body vibrated he knew she teetered on the edge. He enclosed that swollen nub between his lips and lashed it with his tongue until she came in a wet rush, all over his face.

Trevor eased back. Kissing the insides of her thighs. Brushing his mouth between her hipbones. "Chass?"

"Hang on. Let me get my brain back online."

He laughed. He stood and ran his hands down the lean length of her body. "Take your time."

"But not too much time," Edgard said from the doorway.

A shudder worked down Trevor's body at the hungry look on Edgard's face.

****

"Why you still wearing clothes?" Trevor asked.

"Got distracted watching you two."

Chassie pushed up on her elbows and looked at Edgard. "Since Ed's the only one dressed, I think he oughta give us a strip tease."

"You heard her."

"Bein' a mite bossy for a man I'm about to bend over a chair and fuck hard."

Trevor crossed his arms over his chest. "I'll act submissive if it'll get you nekkid faster."

Edgard flashed a predatory smile. "You bein' submissive to me won't be an act." He unsnapped the pearl buttons one at a time until his entire chest was exposed. He shrugged out of the shirt, letting it flutter to the floor. He turned on his heel and walked into the living room.

Behind him he heard the bed squeak and the crack of skin on flesh, followed by Chassie's yelp. Yeah, he'd wanted to smack that smooth butt of hers too.

He paused between the coffee table and the recliner. When Chassie and Trevor appeared, he pointed to the chair. "That's where you are, sweet Chass."

"Cool. No matter where you guys end up, I've got a front row seat." Her tits bounced nicely when she dropped in the chair. "Ooh and you already set the vibrators out. Thoughtful."

"I try." Edgard sat on the edge of the coffee table and stretched his legs out. "How about you get on your knees..." He grinned. "And start by takin' my boots off?"

Trevor ambled over and dropped to his knees. He cupped his palm beneath the heel of Edgard's right boot and tugged. He threw the boot behind him and reached for Edgard's left foot. One tug and that boot joined the other. Socks were next. Then Trevor crawled between his legs. He placed his hands beside Edgard's on the coffee table and got in Edgard's face. "Do I gotta ask permission before I kiss you?"

"You just did."

"God I love this mouth. I can't get enough of it." Trevor's lips were soft and yielding, not at all the brutal, impatient kiss Edgard had expected. As Trevor continued to blow his mind with the seductive glide of lips on lips, his hands went to Edgard's belt. He unbuckled and unzipped him without changing the dreamy quality of the kiss.

Trevor eased his lips back to say, "Lift your hips."

Edgard pressed upward, his pelvis bumping into Trevor's.

Trevor dragged Edgard's jeans down and off. He hooked his fingers into Edgard's boxer briefs and pulled them off. "Guess I like stripping you better than you stripping for me."

"That works." Edgard's breath caught when Trevor's callused hands roamed over his chest and belly while that hot mouth attacked his left nipple, stopping to trace the tattoo on his left pectoral. He chanced a quick look at Chassie to see she'd started stroking herself.

Trevor sucked and bit and used his skilled tongue on Edgard's upper body, knowing the places that made him moan, made him hard and made him beg. Keeping his sexy blue-eyed gaze on Edgard's, he kissed down his torso. He stopped when the wet tip of Edgard's cock bumped his chin. "Tell me what you want."

"Take me deep in your throat and hold me there. Like I had Chassie do to you."

A half-growl rumbled from Trevor a second before he sucked Edgard's cock into his mouth. Each bob of Trevor's head pulled the shaft deeper. The tip bumping his soft palate, gliding back over his tongue and teeth, then past the gag reflex until his full lips circled the root of Edgard's cock. "I love it when you're on your knees and my dick is buried in your mouth."

Trevor swallowed in response.

Edgard groaned. "Again."

He complied. Then he released Edgard's cock slowly. "Scoot to the edge."

The instant Edgard moved, Trevor sucked Edgard's sac. That deep suctioning tug caused Edgard to moan. Then that wicked tongue slipped down and back to lap at his asshole. "Jesus."

"You love this." Trevor teased the pucker with wet swirls before pushing his tongue into the hole, fucking him with short jabs.

"God. Damn."

Trevor slid his hands up Edgard's thighs. "Turn around and brace your hands on the coffee table. I need a better angle."

Edgard stood on shaking legs, widening his stance as Trevor grabbed hold of each butt cheek, squeezing and caressing as he tongued him straight to heaven.

"You two should see how hot you look during a rim job. So fuckin' sexy. Gets me off every time." The buzz of the vibrator got louder.

Trevor didn't pause at all in his licking, tongue thrusting and the soft smooches. He just drove Edgard out of his fucking mind with the erotic way his mouth worked him.

Chassie gasped and emitted a series of breathy moans, her eyes locked on them as she masturbated herself to orgasm.

Then Trevor's lips followed the crack of Edgard's ass, up his spine, to his nape. Edgard loved the feel of Trevor's full weight on him, pinning him down. Trevor pushed his erection between Edgard's balls and rubbed their cocks together.

"You sure you don't want me to fuck you?" Trevor murmured in his ear.

"Later. Grab the lube."

Trevor lifted up, giving Edgard one hip slap before moving.

"You want me to use that crop on you, Trev?"

He laughed. "You'd have to wrestle me for it and we both know how that always turns out. Where are we doin' this?"

When he turned around, holding the lube, Edgard was right there. "On the floor. I want rug burns on your knees so you remember who put them there."

A dark look entered Trevor's eyes. "Like I could ever forget, *amigo*. Who you are to me, what you do to me. Inside and out."

"Sweet words won't get you sweet lovin', my man." Edgard kissed him hard and snatched the lube. "Hands and knees."

Trevor dropped to the carpet. Edgard heard Chassie move behind them. He squirted a generous amount of lube on his fingers and coated his cock. He reached out and smacked Trevor's ass. "Tilt your hips up."

"And you called me Mr. Bossy," he said to Chassie, who'd perched on the edge of the coffee table, vibrator in hand, to watch.

Chassie snorted. "You love it when he's like this."

"So do you," he pointed out.

Edgard added more lube to his fingers and smeared it around Trevor's asshole. Pushing one finger inside, he rubbed the tip across Trevor's prostate as his mouth worshiped Trevor's strong back. He loved the way the muscles bunched and relaxed beneath his tongue and teeth. He loved that beneath Trevor's musky scent, Edgard could still smell Chassie on his skin.

"How long you gonna tease me?" Trevor demanded.

"As long as I want." More lube, another finger, and Edgard was about to burst out of his skin with the need to get inside that tight ass.

He poised his cock at the soft pucker and said, "I wanna hear you as I fuck you," and rammed his cock deep on the first thrust.

Trevor groaned.

"That's it." His balls swung forward with every hard snap of his hips. Feeling the squeeze of that narrow passage as he withdrew completely. Circling the tip around that stretched opening and slamming in fully over and over.

Edgard curled his hands around Trevor's shoulders to give himself leverage. He canted his hips, dragging his cock over Trevor's prostate on every pass.

And his man loved it rough like this. He made masculine-sounding whimpers, but they were whimpers nonetheless.

Edgard looked down, watching his cock pounding into Trevor's ass. And what an ass. Round, high and firm. The man filled out a pair of Wranglers and then some.

He tried to stave off his orgasm, because it felt so fucking good. He layered his chest to Trevor's back. His pelvis pumping, his mouth grazing Trevor's ear. "I can go another ten minutes if I slow down and have my hips do all the work."

"No, goddamn you. I wanna hear you come. I want the satisfaction of knowing what I do to you."

Edgard grinned and licked the shell of his ear. "I lied. I'll be lucky if I last another ten seconds as I'm about to blow. Are you hard again?"

"Fuck yes. Every time you do that..." Trevor's words were lost on a moan as Edgard did the twisting maneuver with his hips anyway.

A sheen of sweat covered them both. Edgard wanted to flip Trevor on his back, push his legs up by his ears and look into his gorgeous face as he pumped into him. But his orgasm was too close. His need too sharp this first time.

He pushed upright again and gripped Trevor's waist, pulling his body back to meet every hard thrust. "Chass," he panted. "Be ready."

"You should see his face, Edgard," she said softly. "So lost to what you're doin' to him."

That tipped him over the edge.

Trevor's channel clamped down on Edgard's cock as he started to come. "Give it to me. Harder."

He roared as he poured every bit of hot seed into Trevor until his balls were drained.

Shadows wavered in the sunlight, dancing across his face in a strobe-light effect, giving the moment a surreal, dreamlike quality. He had a temporary sense of panic that this wasn't real. But the rhythmic clasp of Trevor's ass around his cock, the heat and hardness of his lover's body beneath him, and Chassie's soft hand caressing his shoulder grounded him. Reminding him this wasn't a dream. This was his life. Their life.

Edgard grabbed hold of Trevor's hair and cranked his head around so he could take his mouth. "I love you," he said between ferocious kisses. "So fucking much."

"I know." Trevor gave those ravenous kisses right back to him. "I need…"

Then Chassie was there, her chest against Trevor's, her mouth working the cords straining in his throat. "I know what you need." She slipped her hands between Edgard and Trevor's bodies to where they were still joined. Pressing her thumbs into Edgard's hips she pushed him back.

Edgard eased out of the tight heat slowly. Before Trevor could pin Chassie to the floor and plow into her like a madman, Edgard grabbed her chin, forcing her to look at him. "Hands and knees for you too, baby."

She turned around and Trevor caged her small body beneath his, his hips pumping ferociously as he fucked her. He threw his head back and shouted, his body shuddering as he came.

As soon as Trevor's body stilled, Edgard crawled in front of Chassie. He placed the vibrator directly on her clit. "Now come for me." He swallowed her surprised gasp in a consuming kiss, and didn't back off until she unraveled between them again.

They all three slumped to the floor in a sweaty, sticky, spent pile. After they'd caught their breath Chassie asked, "So how are we gonna spend the rest of the day?"

****

A few hours later, after exploring the outdoor area and another round of hot sex, they put on robes and returned to the kitchen to cook supper.

Trevor had gotten better over the years with cooking. He grilled a mean steak. While he manned the grill, Edgard fried potatoes and heated a frozen bag of corn.

"I feel useless," Chassie complained.

"Then set the table. I think there are actual glass glasses in the cabinet."

"How will we get through dinner with no plastic cartoon cups?"

After all the food was on the table, they looked at each other and grinned. "Well ain't this fancy."

"No ketchup or ranch dressing. And we don't have to cut up anyone's food."

"Even our picky eater Sophia would've eaten this," Trevor mused.

"The steak is cooked perfectly, Trev."

He smirked at Edgard. "I know exactly how you like your meat."

They snickered like twelve-year-old boys and Chassie rolled her eyes.

The silence as they ate was nice for a change, since mealtimes at home were always loud.

"I can't remember the last time we had a meal in our robes," Chassie said.

Trevor swallowed a mouthful of beer. "Maybe when you were tryin' to get pregnant that first time and we were goin' at it everywhere, all the time?"

"Yeah, probably not a good thing to tell Westin that he was conceived in the dining room."

Edgard noticed Chassie had been picking at her corn more than eating it. "Something wrong, *querida?*"

"I'm happy to be here alone with you guys, but I'll admit I do miss the kids."

"So do we, sweetheart." Trevor reached for her hand. "I know it'll put your mind at ease to call them before bedtime to see how they're doin'." She lifted his hand and kissed it. "Thank you. Now that that's out of the way, what else do you have planned for tonight?"

Edgard wiped his mouth and set his napkin aside. "We brought a couple of movies—non-cartoon stuff we've been wanting to watch but don't have time for."

"Or we could play cribbage," Trevor offered.

"Or we could just pile onto the couch and watch TV."

"How would that be any different than a night at home?" Chassie asked.

"Max wouldn't be running around yelling, 'Mama, Mama watch me,' while he's throwing toys everywhere," Trevor said dryly.

Edgard nodded. "And we wouldn't be checking Westin's homework, finishing laundry, working on scheduling goat milk transportation and cattle shipment times, while combing out Sophia's hair and wrestling Max and Westin into the tub—"

"Okay, okay, I get it. Tonight will be more sedate," Chassie said, standing and carrying her plate to the sink.

"Plus, we won't have to share our popcorn with the little popcorn hogs." Edgard hip-checked her away from the sink. "The movies are in the bag in the bedroom. Pick one while Trev and I finish the dishes."

"You guys cooked and are cleaning up? I really am on vacation."

Trevor snapped her ass with a dishtowel. "Keep it up, smarty-pants and you will feel that crop tonight."

After stowing the leftovers in the fridge, Edgard filled the sink with water and washed while Trevor dried.

"There's something I forgot to mention after all that bullshit happened with Westin at school. I ran into Colby earlier that day when I was picking up groceries. He asked if Westin was entered in the mutton bustin' event at the 4-H fundraiser next weekend."

Edgard looked at him. "What'd you say?"

"That we'd talk about it. But to be honest, I don't wanna bring it up unless Westin asks us about it."

"Why?"

"Because I'm not sure I want him involved in the sport of rodeo at all." Trevor leaned against the counter. "You know my Dad didn't give me a choice. And with you and me bein' on the circuit as professionals, I don't want Westin to feel he's gotta live up to something that we only enjoyed the last few years because we got to be together."

"You're afraid he thinks we'll be disappointed in him if he doesn't at least try it and carry on some kind of family tradition in rodeo?"

Trevor nodded. "Or worse...what if he tries it and likes it? I mean, we both just disappeared off the circuit. But guaranteed if Westin starts ropin', his last name will create interest. Which will lead to buzz, rumors, and all that bullshit we're tryin' to avoid. Especially when folks in the rodeo world learn that you changed your last name to Glanzer and we're living together with Chassie West. That'll bring up Dag, too." He shifted his stance. "I'm not ashamed of our life, but we do keep a low profile. Putting our kid in the rodeo arena probably ain't the best thing to keep it that way."

Edgard frowned. "I don't disagree. Has Westin expressed interest in rodeoin' to you?"

"He mentioned his cousins—Colby's, Cord's and Cam's boys—are competing in a few events this fall."

"That's it?"

Trevor's eyes narrowed. "Yeah. Why?"

"Sounds to me like he was testing the waters to see what you'd say. We can point out that it's doubtful Colt and Indy will let their boys compete. Westin worships Boone and Boone ain't a rodeo cowboy, so we can add that too."

"Jesus, Ed, you're missing the point."

"No, I'm not." Edgard closed the distance between them. "You are. If he wants to try it, we'll let him try it. If we tell him no, he's gonna want to do it even more. Much as we'd like to plan for every variable in our kids' lives, we can't."

Trevor hooked the towel around Edgard's neck and tugged. "You are one smart bastard." He smashed his lips to Edgard's in a punishing kiss.

Edgard lightly punched Trevor in the gut to break the lip lock. "Come on. Let's get these dishes done."

"Should we bring this up with Chassie?" Trevor asked softly.

"Not unless Westin expresses real interest in the sport. Our Chass worries enough as it is. And with what happened at school this week... well, I say leave it be. Let's focus on why we're here this weekend."

Trevor grinned. "Sex. Lots and lots of sex."

A loud, "Omigod, are you serious?" echoed from the bedroom.

"Looks like she found the movies."

"Hey, man, I'm blaming you that the only thing we brought was porn."

****

Later the next afternoon they were lazing in bed after a long and sweaty bout of sex. There'd been a certain sweetness having Edgard between them. Edgard making love to Chassie slowly from behind, whispering Portuguese against her neck as Trevor fucked Edgard at the same leisurely pace, his mouth and hands in constant motion on both of them.

So basking in the afterglow between her men was the perfect time to state her intent. "I wanna have another baby."

Both her men propped up on an elbow and looked at her. "Why?"

"We talked about havin' four kids. If we are serious, I want to do it soon. Max is already two."

"Like how soon, sweetheart?" Trevor asked.

"I go in next month for my annual checkup. I'd like to get my IUD taken out."

"If we had another baby, the kids would outnumber us," Edgard said. "Our little Max is a handful. More so than Westin and Sophia put together. Makes me wonder what kind of hellion kid four would be."

Trevor chuckled and Chassie elbowed him in the gut.

"I'm serious. I miss havin' a baby in the house. I think about holding one, rocking one, how good they smell and seeing that sweet little happy face first thing every morning."

"You're forgetting the lack of sleep, the constant crying, one of us always bein' tethered at home, and Chass, that's usually you. Plus, we've still got Max in diapers."

Chassie's gaze moved from Trevor's face to Edgard's. "You're both against it?"

"No," they said simultaneously. "I just think we oughta make sure you wanna have another baby for the right reasons," Trevor said.

"Meaning what?"

"You tell us." Edgard's golden-brown eyes were so serious.

"This has nothin' to do with what that shithead said to Westin at school this week," she retorted.

"You sure?"

"Positive." She placed a hand on each of their cheeks. "We make beautiful, smart, compassionate human beings. It's been shown to us time and time again that the world could use more kids like ours. Especially where we live."

"Such a sweet talker," Trevor drawled.

"That she is," Edgard agreed.

"Besides, I really feel that one more child would make our family complete."

Trevor and Edgard exchanged a look.

"Stop *doin'* that," she said poking them both in the chest. "You have something to say, spit it out."

"Do you feel like you need to even it up for my benefit?" Trevor asked. "Because biologically, two of our kids are Edgard's and one is mine?"

"No!" Chassie inhaled. Exhaled. "Okay, maybe. Look, the only reason we had paternity tests done was to set up the legal guardianship in case something happened to one of us or two of us, so there wasn't any chance the kids could get separated by the courts. We've never treated any of the kids like anything but ours—*all* of ours. And when we were tryin' to get pregnant, we let nature take its course—no selective breeding."

Edgard groaned and Trevor laughed.

"But this time, if we decide we're all on board havin' another baby, I would like for Trev to have first crack at providing the fastest swimmers." She leaned over and kissed each of them. "I love you both. I wanna have another baby with you both. I just wanted to bring this up before my appointment and when we don't have kids underfoot."

"Because that might change our minds about adding another one to the chaos?" Edgard said dryly.

"Not funny." Chassie flicked his chest.

"One thing I'd like to point out is if we do add to our family, we'll also need to add to our house. We're busting out of the bedrooms upstairs. And bein' here," Edgard gestured to the generous space around them, "just shows that I wouldn't mind havin' a bigger place like this for us all the time."

Trevor scratched his chin, a faraway look in his eyes. "You know, I have been thinking about this. If we added a master suite off the living room, we'd have to install plumbing for the big bathroom with a gigantic shower that I know Chass is dyin' to have."

"Hey, I heard the two of you enjoying the gigantic shower here yesterday. Really enjoying it."

"You were sleeping. We were bored."

"Oh, you gotta be bored to fuck me, Brazil nut? That's reassuring."

Edgard leaned over and kissed Trevor. "Chass just attested to the fact I enjoyed it, so lose the pout."

Some days Chassie found it hard to believe there was no jealousy between the three of them. From the start they'd made certain that even the smallest perceived slight would be addressed by all of them immediately.

Although they spent the majority of their time in and out of bed as a trio, they also made sure they got couple time too—her with each of them individually and them with each other. No one ever got the short end of the stick, in love, in bed, in parenting, or in being an equal member of the household. She was so very thankful every day that it worked.

She tuned back into the conversation as Trevor said, "Since we're already adding new plumbing, then we could add a ground floor laundry room, which would make everything easier."

Edgard nodded. "Then we could finish the basement, wall off a bedroom or two and turn it into a kids' area, since our dining room and living room are bein' overrun with toys."

Trevor pushed a hank of Chassie's hair over her shoulder. "I agree with Ed. I think it's time we had a bigger space for the three of us. We're conscious of kids overhearing when we're getting down and dirty, so creating a separate area would give us privacy."

"I agree. I'll give Chet and Remy a call."

"Why don't you let me do it?" Trevor asked. "There's a lot me'n Ed can do ourselves and that'll affect the cost, even with the West family discount."

"So does that mean yes to another baby?"

"Like we'd ever say no to you. It helps your case that you're such an outstanding mama. And that you're not a psycho pregnant woman," Edgard said.

"But childbirth does take a toll on my body. Stretch marks on my tits, my ass, my belly and my hips. Not to mention I turn into a nympho or act like a nun—with no options in between."

"The stretch marks are beautiful to me," Trevor said softly.

"And to me," Edgard said. He traced the jagged white lines beneath her left breast. "You fed our babies with these, Chass. It's an amazing thing your body can do. It should show the changes because you've—we've all—changed with each child." Then his fingers followed the intertwined the letters C, T and E tattoo centered above her left breast—the exact same tattoo both he and Trevor had in the exact same spot on their bodies.

"I loved how round you got with each pregnancy." Trevor let his fingers drag across her lower belly. "It's a miracle. Three miracles. So don't ever think we're lookin' at you with anything besides love, admiration and lust. It's humbling what this body can still do to me every time I look at you or touch it."

"Same here, *querida*. Mr. Smooth said it all right for a change."

Chassie closed her eyes...overwhelmed by her love for them.

Trevor gathered her against his chest. "Hey. No cryin' allowed. Why don't we all just stay right here and nap for a little longer? There's no reason to get up."

"Sounds good. So we don't have any big plans for tonight?" she asked with a yawn.

"We do have a few movies left to watch," Trevor said.

"Right, we didn't make it through the first one before we were all on each other."

"You say that like it's a bad thing."

"It's not. But, man, it's been a few years since we've gone at it this hard." Edgard kissed her eyelids. "So you'd probably better rest up, huh?"

****

The next morning Chassie had managed to shampoo her hair and shave before she was joined in the big shower by both her men.

"You know, we've been talkin'," Trevor started.

Her gaze zeroed in on their crotches, one at a time. "Looks like you've been doin' more than talkin'."

Edgard poured body wash in his hands and created lather. Then he began soaping the front side of her body, starting at her collarbones. His soft, sure lips moved from the tip of her chin up the side of her jaw.

Her entire body became a mass of gooseflesh.

Then Trevor's body was snugged up behind hers, his mouth on her ear. "We had plans for you this morning before we have to leave."

"But this will work too," Edgard murmured in her other ear.

"So just relax and let us take care of you." Trevor's mouth skated along the arch of her neck.

Chassie sighed and closed her eyes. She loved everything about the three of them being together, but when they double-teamed her like this, focused entirely on her pleasure, well, it reminded her of how lucky she was.

Slippery hands caressed her body, front and back.

"I love how your skin smells. Not only because you use this honey, goat's milk, and lavender body wash."

"It is pretty cool that Sky Blue uses so much of our goat milk in their products. I never thought I could make such a good living selling—"

"Really, Chass? We're all three nekkid together in this shower and you're talking business?" Trevor admonished with mock outrage.

She laughed. "I'm sorry. I surrender to you both completely."

"Good choice," Edgard whispered, sending goose bumps cascading down her body. "Close your eyes. Let us take care of you."

Every touch, every kiss, sent her deeper into that fuzzy white void where they owned her completely. She trusted them with everything she had, with everything she was.

"Hands on the wall, sweetheart."

Trevor entered her from behind, angling her slightly forward as she braced herself against the shower wall. His hands continued that constant stroking as he slid in and out of her pussy; his mouth busy teasing the back of her neck.

Then Edgard dropped to his knees.

Her knees nearly buckled when his tongue began tracing her slit, top to bottom, circling her clit. "Oh God this feels so good."

When Trevor pulled out and paused, she felt Edgard's tongue licking the head of Trevor's cock, then switching to swirl his tongue around the opening to her sex.

Trevor growled against her nape, slowing down so Edgard could tease them both.

Chassie started to drift, the steam from the shower returning her to that hazy state, Trevor sending her to another plane with his mouth, his hands and his cock.

When Edgard zigzagged his tongue back up her slit, her belly performed a slow, delicious roll. He spread the fleshy skin covering her clit and settled his mouth there until she came against his flickering tongue and sucking lips.

Her body still was quaking when Edgard stood and pulled her against him. Mashed between two wet, hard male bodies caused her sex to clench around Trevor's hard shaft.

Edgard and Trevor shared a long, sexy kiss.

After Edgard pulled away, Trevor growled, "She tastes good on you."

Chassie curled her hands around Edgard's face.

"I need to fuck you, Chass," he said against her lips. "With Trev. Right here, right now."

"Yes. Please."

Trevor pulled out of her body and backed away.

Before she lodged a protest, Edgard said, "Jump up. Legs around my waist." Grabbing her butt cheeks, he gave her a boost. Then they were indulging in those drugging kisses.

Chassie threaded her hands through Edgard's dark hair, holding him close and tight enough to feel his heart pounding against hers.

A cool and slippery finger circled her anus as a warm mouth sucked the droplets of water from her shoulder. Then the slick digit pressed against the opening and slipped inside.

Trevor's breaths were short and choppy across her skin as he worked more lube into her ass, using two fingers. "Ready to take both of us, sweetheart?"

"Always." A tingle of anticipation unfurled low in her belly as they aligned their cocks.

Both men released a hiss of pleasure when the tips of their cocks rubbed together. They pushed inside her with a simultaneous thrust. She moaned, loving that immediate feeling of fullness with a sharp bite of pain.

"You feel so good, Chassie," Trevor murmured in her ear. "Tight and hot."

"Warm and wet," Edgard added in her other ear.

Trevor moved and Edgard countered the move. Slow, slow, slow and then four rapid-fire thrusts as he bottomed out in her ass. Edgard would keep the same maddeningly steady pace...and then jackhammer into her pussy like a man possessed.

Chassie's entire body was awash in sensation. Inside. Outside. Hands, mouths, cocks. Teeth on her skin. Fingers pinching her nipples. The muscular heat of Trevor's body behind her. The grinding thrusts of Edgard's pelvis against her clit. She was suspended between them. Bent to their will. Their bodies working in tandem and in opposition to make her fly apart.

Edgard kissed her. Then Trevor angled her head to kiss her. Then three mouths met and it shouldn't have worked, but it did. It was erotic as hell.

"Come on, baby, I know it's right there," Edgard panted. "I can feel your body vibrating. You know how this goes. We don't come until you come."

"I know what'll get her there." Trevor grabbed a fistful of her wet hair and pulled.

The sharp sting on her scalp and Trevor's mouth sucking on the spot below her ear was like a jolt of electricity. She arched and cried out, "Harder. Faster. So close."

The sounds of their heavy breathing bounced off the shower walls as their cocks powered into her, creating the most amazing friction.

Chassie drew one breath before she unraveled. Her cunt spasmed around Edgard's cock and her anal muscles clamped down on Trevor's shaft. The throbbing pulses so intense she held her breath. As the last twinge faded, twin grunts echoed. Trevor's pelvis slammed into her butt as he spilled heat in her ass.

Edgard's cock remained buried deep, his hips bumping short jabs as he came in hot spurts.

Trevor rested his forehead on her right shoulder and Edgard rested his forehead on her left shoulder. Her pulse still raced and her body quaked from aftershocks when she kissed Trevor's temple and then Edgard's. "That was...spectacular. Thank you." She whispered, "I love you," to each man, nuzzling ears and necks.

They lifted their heads and looked at each other with cocky grins.

"I definitely think we need to build a shower like this at home."

CHAPTER THREE

Two days after returning to Sundance, Chassie was cleaning Max up after lunch, when the phone rang. Caller ID said, *Moorcroft Elem*. She answered quickly. "Hello?"

"Mrs. Glanzer? This is Patricia Donkle. I'm the school counselor."

"What happened to Westin?"

"He was involved in an altercation on the playground. He hit another student."

She closed her eyes. "Where is Westin now?"

"He's in my office. I've called the parents of the other student who was involved. School policy is a face-to-face meeting. How soon can you be here?"

"Fifteen or twenty minutes."

"Good. Just check in at the front office."

Chassie hung up. Max had stopped pounding on his high chair tray and looked ready to crash since it was close to his naptime.

Trevor and Sophia bounded in, Sophia chattering a million miles an hour, Edgard bringing up the rear. So it wasn't a surprise that Edgard noticed her distress first.

"Chassie, what's wrong?"

"The school called. Westin has been involved in a playground incident. So the counselor has asked me to come to the school."

"Just now?" Trevor asked.

"Yeah." Her mind raced. "So if you'll get Max down for his nap, I'll go—"

"No. We'll all go." Edgard spoke to Sophia. "Can you get Max's coat?"

"Sure." She skipped off.

"Now you wanna tell us what's really goin' on?"

"I told you everything I know. The other kid's parents will be there." She lifted Max out of the high chair. "Wouldn't it be easier if one of us stayed here with the younger kids?"

"Which one of us stays?" Trevor demanded.

They looked at each other.

"We *all* go," Trevor reiterated.

The ride into town was quiet—even Sophia and Max were subdued.

They traipsed into the school and signed in at the office before being directed down a long hallway. A heavyset woman, probably mid-fifties, exited the office marked Counselor. "Hi, Mrs. Glanzer?"

"Yes."

"I'm Patricia Donkle." The counselor's gaze moved between Edgard and Trevor before returning to Chassie. "And they are?"

"Westin's fathers. Trevor and Edgard Glanzer."

"Oh. That's...good you're all here. We're in these two rooms."

Max had started to fuss so Trevor plucked him out of Chassie's arms and carried him. Sophia remained close to Edgard.

As soon as the door to the conference room opened, Westin ran to Chassie, burying his face against her stomach.

"Hey, sweetie." She tried to push him back but he wouldn't budge; he'd curled himself around her completely. "You all right?"

Westin shook his head.

"Why don't you all have a seat? I'll bring in the other parents."

"We'd prefer if you'd fill us in about what's goin' on first," Edgard said.

Chassie chose a seat at the end of the table and Trevor and Edgard flanked her, keeping the kids on their laps.

"Evidently one of our students has been saying inappropriate things to Westin. A situation none of us were aware of. But I learned today that it's been going on for a couple of days. Isn't that right, Westin?"

He nodded.

"The boy is two grades older and Westin had been ignoring him, but things escalated today. Westin, would you please tell your parents what happened?"

Westin kept his gaze focused on the carpet. "Robbie followed me around the playground yelling that my family was all faggots. So I punched him. And I'm not sorry. I'm not! He's mean." He dissolved into tears again.

Cassie looked to Edgard and Trevor for support. They were as shocked as she. None of them knew what to say.

"So, you understand why we need to deal with this matter as soon as possible."

"Of course." Chassie pulled Westin away from where he was clinging to her neck.

The counselor opened the adjoining door.

A man, woman and young boy entered, taking seats as far from them as possible.

The woman's lip curled as she looked at the three of them. She turned her head and whispered behind her hand in her husband's ear.

The pudgy boy knuckled away a tear and glared at Westin.

"Mr. and Mrs. Feckling have demanded Westin apologize to Robbie."

Chassie's arms tightened around Westin. "Westin will apologize as long as Robbie also apologizes."

"For what?" Mrs. Feckling demanded. "That boy hit my son."

"And your son bullied mine. On more than one occasion."

"This is outrageous." Mrs. Feckling addressed the counselor. "An apology is off the table. We want that little freak suspended from school. Who knows what else might set him off and he'll start swinging again."

"Your son has been calling Westin's family horrid names for several days, Mrs. Feckling."

"That doesn't give him the right to use his fists."

"Not even to defend himself against a bigger, meaner boy?" Chassie snapped.

"Maybe he should grow thicker skin," the woman sneered. "Robbie didn't say anything that isn't true." Her piggy-eyed gaze moved between Chassie, Edgard and Trevor and she shuddered. "You live a perverted lifestyle."

"Our lifestyle isn't the issue here," Edgard said. "The fact of the matter is your son is a bully. And I'll bet this is not the first time you've been called into the school to deal with his behavior." He looked at the counselor and she nodded.

Mr. Feckling said nothing as Mrs. Feckling kept yapping. "What gives you the right to question our—"

"I've heard enough out of you. Cut to the chase," Trevor said to the school counselor, cutting off Mrs. Feckling's diatribe. "What happens now?"

"We have a zero-tolerance policy for violence, so Westin is looking at a two-day suspension from school."

"Praise the Lord something makes sense around here." Mrs. Feckling patted Robbie's shoulder. "See? I told you we'd handle it."

Robbie smirked.

Chassie wasn't mad at the kid; he couldn't help being a bully, a bigot and a homophobe since he was being raised by one.

The counselor faced Robbie's parents. "Since the start of the school year we've also enacted a zero-tolerance policy for bullying, so your son will also be suspended for two days."

"What? My son is punished for stating a truth? Look at them! That's unnatural. It's obvious they're f—"

"I will caution you, Mrs. Feckling, to refrain from repeating the offensive language that your son used," the counselor warned. "I will also remind you that just because previous complaints about your son bullying other children have been officially withdrawn, the unofficial incidents are on your son's permanent record. If he keeps it up he might end up suspended for the entire year."

"So that little"—she pointed at Westin—"freak gets preferential treatment?"

"Call my son a name again and I'll show you exactly where he learned to punch," Chassie said flatly.

Edgard and Trevor each put a hand on her thigh under the table. Thoughtful and supportive, but it wouldn't hold her back from kicking ass if need be.

"Mrs. Glanzer, I know emotions are high right now, but threatening violence isn't acceptable." She gave Mrs. Feckling a stern look. "If I hear you refer to Westin by anything besides his given name, I will recommend a social services agency visit your home to ascertain whether your son is being verbally abused at home and lashing out with the same type of behavior at school."

"How dare you! Our lawyer—"

"Sharon," Mr. Feckling snapped. "Shut your mouth."

She sent him a dirty look.

"As it sits, both Westin and Robbie will receive a two-day suspension starting tomorrow. They can return to school on Monday, but they must meet with me and the principal before attending class. Any questions?"

Silence.

"Then we're finished." The counselor stood.

So did the Feckling family. "Since we're officially done, just let me say that no one wants this kid or any of your other kids at this school. We're a Christian community and your amoral behavior disgusts us. You think my son speaking his mind is bad? You should hear what some of the other *parents* are saying about you three. I don't see it changing anytime soon."

"Not with attitudes like yours. What about your Christian tenets of *judge not lest ye be judged?*" Chassie asked.

"We have a right to judge because it protects our children from people like you who fly in the face of traditional family values." She offered a smug smile. "And there's only so much the school district can do to protect your child from this type of thing becoming a daily occurrence."

"Is that a threat?" Trevor asked.

"It's a promise." The Fecklings swept out of the room.

Westin turned his head and looked at her. "Mama? Why does she hate us so much?"

"Because she's so full of hate that she doesn't understand love." She kissed his forehead. "Let's go home."

The counselor looked frustrated. "I don't understand people like her, but there are a dozen exactly like her that have kids at this school."

"So you're telling us that Westin might always have a rough go of it here?"

She nodded. "I'm sorry. I hate it. I'm trying to change things, but change is slow. And I feel it's better to be upfront with you."

"Thanks," Trevor said. "We appreciate it."

But Chassie was thinking, *don't be surprised if we aren't here for school come Monday morning.*

****

After they returned home, Chassie and Sophia went to deal with the goats. Edgard took Westin along to check cattle. Max had thrown a screaming fit in the car until he'd crashed from exhaustion. So Trevor was in the house while Max napped, working on BLM land lease renewals.

He'd gone to the kitchen for a cup of coffee when he saw Ramona West pull up.

She immediately bounded up the steps. She smiled at him through the glass door, but her smile dried seeing the tight set to Trevor's face. He let her in. "This is a surprise."

"What's going on?"

"Did Chassie call you?"

"No. I'm leaving tomorrow and I came to say goodbye. Has something happened?"

Trevor was the type who wanted to keep family business in the family. *Ramona has been your family since you married Chassie.*

"Yeah. Have a seat. Want coffee?"

"Nah. I'm good. What's going on?"

Trevor sat across from her. "When you watched the kids last weekend did Westin mention anything that'd been happening at school?"

Ramona nodded. "Nothing specific. Just that some kid was talking smack about his family."

"Did he ask for your advice?"

"No, but I think he wanted to. He's a deliberate thinker, isn't he?"

"Very. But today, he took action and punched the kid who's been bullying him. He got suspended from school. The other kid's mother said a whole bunch of nasty shit to us about our perverted lifestyle. Not only was Westin in the room, so were Sophia and Max."

She reached for his arm and squeezed. "Oh Trevor. I'm sorry. That's horrible."

"So now Chass has it in her head to pull Westin out and homeschool him. Part of me doesn't disagree with that. But there's a part of me thinks it'll be worse for him—for all the kids in the long run if we do that."

"And you're beating yourself up because Westin didn't choose the unconventional lifestyle you live—and he's getting the backlash for it?"

Trevor nodded, not at all shocked she'd hit his worry right on the head. "So maybe it is best to keep them all here until they've developed the skills to deal with them type of people."

"It's easy for me to say *fight it* because I don't have the same life experiences you three have in living the way you do. I don't know how I'd handle looking into Westin's sweet face every day and telling him to suck it up."

"When I think about dropping him off at the bus stop and leaving him to face that shit alone? At age six? I almost break out in hives."

"What about changing schools? Hulett or Sundance? It'd be extra driving, but if Westin was in a happier learning environment, it'd be worth it."

Trevor had suggested it, but Chassie refused to consider it. He'd been frustrated to the point that he'd reminded her that her years going to school in Moorcroft had been shitty too.

"Trevor, have you guys talked about this to anyone?"

"Not yet. We're sort of in that state of denial or whatever." And again, he didn't want anyone in their personal business.

But Ramona did not feel the same. She dialed a number on her cell phone and waited for the person on the other end to pick up. "Colby? It's Ramona. I'm good." She laughed. "I did behave while I was here. One night out with Keely. *One.* That's it, I swear! No, Cam did *not* have to break up a bar fight—Keely and I handled it. Anyway, I stopped by to chat with Chassie before I leave and I heard something really distressing. Westin was suspended from school for standing up to a bully."

"Jesus, Ramona."

She shushed him. "The Glanzer clan is having a hard time with this. Do you have time to swing by and offer your old friends and your cousin some support? Because they sure could use it. Uh-huh. No problem. Bye." She hung up and said, "He'll be here in half an hour. And he's calling Colt."

Trevor wanted to ask what Colby and Colt could do, but the truth was, outside advice might help them. "Thanks for meddling, Ramona."

She laughed. "It's what I do."

"You and Keely went out and whooped it up?"

"Just one night. Jack frowns on her getting too wild."

He grinned. "So that's exactly what she did, huh?"

"Yep. I swear those two fight just so they can make up." She shook her head. "I'll never understand love. Which is why I'm still single, by the way."

"As long as I've got you here, you wanna come clean about why you just 'happened' to be in Wyoming the weekend we need you?"

"Didn't buy that coincidence, huh?"

Trevor shook his head. "I wasn't about to look a gift horse in the mouth either. So what's goin' on?"

"That whole *I don't understand love* thing I was complaining about? It's because I swear I have the worst taste in men." Ramona twirled a section of her hair. "The last guy I dated seemed normal, right? He's rich, he's good-looking, he took an interest in me and my life on a level I've never had. Which should've been a warning sign. Anyway, I broke it off. He wasn't ready for that. He refused to accept it, actually."

"Christ, Ramona, is he stalking you?"

"Sort of." She blew out a breath. "Okay, yeah, he's stalking me. Everyone thinks I'm being stupid, that I just don't understand how a real love relationship works, because I'm more the one- or two-night stand kinda chick. But this? This is creepy as hell.

"He follows me everywhere and he doesn't bother with stealth. He sends me gifts—ridiculously expensive gifts." Ramona shot him a look. "Every girl's dream, right? Wrong. I have no way of returning them to the store or the courier service that delivered them. And that's exactly what he wants; me to come to him. That'll add to his delusion I can't keep away from him because we're soul mates."

"How long has this been goin' on?"

"Months. We dated for about three months before I broke it off. He's spent the last six months doing this shit. I went to market in China for two weeks and when I came home? He'd had my bedroom redecorated to match his."

Trevor's jaw dropped. "Are you fuckin' kidding me?"

"No. He's so...smooth and charming he convinced the building manager to give him access to my apartment so he could surprise me." She shuddered. "I put all the bedding in the trash—I made sure he knew I did it. Then I called the Salvation Army to haul away the furniture. That's when I leapt at the chance to come here. I've been traveling on business the last month and I'm actually a little afraid to go home."

"Ramona. Sweetheart. You have to call the cops."

She shook her head. "And tell them what? This man who looks perfect on paper is a psychopath? He's a respected businessman, Trevor."

"Did you talk to your folks? Or your brothers? Or your cousins about this?"

She groaned. "Yes, I told Keely and she tattled to Cam. He freaked out. My God he is one scary-ass dude when he's upset. I shudder to think what he'll be like when Liesl starts dating. Anyway, he's got an old Army buddy who lives in Seattle and he's picking me up at the airport tomorrow. Part of me is pissed because I don't want a damn babysitter. But another part of me is really relieved."

"I'm relieved too. Keep in touch with us, okay?"

"I will. Now tell me about this addition Chet and Remy are putting on."

****

When Edgard and Westin returned home, three vehicles, belonging to Colby, Colt and Ramona were parked in the drive.

"*Papai*, why are there people here?"

"No idea. Let's go find out."

Westin hesitated to get out of the truck.

"Something wrong?" He'd been his same helpful self during the cattle check, hopping out to open gates. He'd been quiet, but that was to be expected, given the day he'd had. So far they hadn't addressed the "hitting is always wrong" issue—mostly because they weren't sure it was wrong in this case. It'd forced everyone to deal with the issue—not just poor Westin alone.

"Do you think I should do pages in my workbook tonight since I'm kicked out of school?"

"Afraid you'll fall behind?" he teased. "Of course you should do it. I'll check it. That means I'll expect the answers in English and Portuguese."

Westin grinned and rattled off "I'll show you" in Portuguese before he jumped out.

Inside the house Colby and Colt sat at the dining room table with Trevor.

"Hey, we've been waiting on you," Trevor said.

"Where's Chass?"

"She and Ramona are havin' a tea party with Max and Sophia. Westin is supposed to go up and Chassie will come down so we can chat a bit."

Westin groaned. "A tea party? Dad, do I have to?"

"Yep. Aunt Ramona mentioned playing Legos afterward."

He tore off.

Colt chuckled. "The L word works every time, doesn't it?"

Trevor kicked out the chair next to him. "Have a seat."

Edgard noticed no one was drinking beer. Much as he could use one, he'd wait. Colt had been sober for years, but he respected the man too much to make him uncomfortable.

"Word of warning? Don't ask what the powwow is about—that'll get Chass's back up."

"Christ, Trev, did you really say that to her?"

"Once. She told me if I ever said it again she'd whap me upside the head with a cast iron skillet and then fill my ass with buckshot."

Colt and Colby laughed.

Chassie sauntered in. "What's so funny?"

"Nothin', sweetheart, have a seat."

She sat next to Trevor and blurted, "So Ramona called you?"

Colby nodded. "I'm glad she did 'cause I know you wouldn't have." His gaze encompassed all of them. "None of you would have. And that's bullshit. We're family."

"I know what it's like to want to fight your own battles," Colt said, "but I also know when you need to ask for help."

"How can you help us?"

Edgard reached for Chassie's hand. "They're helpin' us just by bein' here."

She relaxed.

"So Sassy Chassie," Colt started and grinned, "why in the hell would you send your kid to school in Moorcroft anyway? Because that's where you went? As I recall, your school years were awful."

"But I thought my experience might've just been me. My issue bein' ethnic and poor. And Westin had a wonderful kindergarten teacher. The parents in his class seemed to like us and accept us." Her nose wrinkled. "Well, most of them."

Edgard looked at Colt. "You're in the Moorcroft school district too. Doesn't Hudson start kindergarten next year?"

"Yeah, but he's goin' to school in Sundance. That's always been the plan."

"Really?" Trevor asked. "Why?"

"Two reasons. The bus picks the kids up so damn early. There's no reason for them to have to wait an hour to get to school and an hour to get home."

Chassie gave Edgard a sheepish smile. "That's what Ed said."

"Smart man. The other reason is all Hudson's cousins go to school in Sundance. There's no mornin' bus service, but Indy or I have to go to town anyway. And I know the kids; they watch out for each other." Colt leaned over and poked Chassie's arm. "Just like they would if Westin went to school with them."

"Before you got here, Ramona was telling me how much she hated that you, she and Keely all went to different schools," Trevor said.

"Where did Ramona go?" Edgard asked.

"Hulett."

Colby leaned forward. "I'm gonna be blunt here, guys, okay? The worst thing you could do to Westin is pull him out of public school and homeschool him. Kids need friends and activities outside their siblings, parents and home environment. If you keep him sheltered, you've got no chance to prove to the people who think your situation is fucked up, that there's nothin' wrong with it."

Edgard had forgotten how intuitive Colby was. The man defined pragmatic and loyal. The three of them had shared good times during the years they traveled the rodeo circuit together. Edgard knew Trevor missed that close friendship.

But the fact he was here showed he cared. Edgard would talk with Cassie and Trevor about inviting Colby and Channing and their brood over. Maybe they had isolated themselves more than they'd realized.

"When you put it that way...I definitely don't think we should home-school. My ranting was a knee-jerk reaction." Chassie sighed. "Maybe Westin will have homework if we send him to school in Sundance. He complains now he doesn't have any."

Colby grinned. "Gib was the same way. Braxton...we practically have to hogtie that kid to the chair to get him to finish his schoolwork."

Trevor pointed at Colby. "He gets that from you, pard. We were both the same way."

"True. I'm lucky my former schoolteacher wife cracks the whip on the boys."

"So did any of this convince you to send Westin to school in Sundance?" Colt asked.

The three of them looked at each other. Trevor spoke. "We'll talk about it tonight and make our decision. I'm pretty sure Westin will be on board with it. We appreciate you both comin' and setting us straight."

"That's what family does, dumbass."

Everyone pushed back from the table.

"If you do decide to transfer him, give me a heads up. Me'n Chan will meet you at the school early on Monday."

Edgard clapped Colby on the back. "Will do. You and your lovely wife and kids oughta come over for supper sometime in the next few weeks."

Colby gave him a big smile. "That'd be great. I'll talk to her."

"When is Channing due again?" Chassie asked.

"We've got a ways to go since she's only three months along."

"Six kids. Man, how're you gonna do that?" Edgard asked.

"No clue. But hell, it's that third kid that's the killer. After that?" He shrugged. "No big."

"We ain't testing that theory," Colt said. "Three is enough because Ellison gets into enough trouble for two kids."

"Didja ever find out why he smeared McKenna with peanut butter?" Trevor asked.

Colt sighed. "He wanted to see if the dog would lick it off her. McKenna was so happy to have Ellison's attention she just sat there and let him do it."

Chassie snickered. "I know it's not funny...the kid looks like an angel but he has such a devilish streak."

"We're gonna hafta keep an eye on Max and Ellison when they start school."

Ramona came downstairs with the kids.

After goodbyes were exchanged, Edgard glanced at the clock. The kids would be asking about supper soon and neither he nor Chassie had made anything.

"Listen up. Get your shoes on and grab your coats. We're goin' out for pizza."

Didn't have to tell them twice. Pizza out usually meant a special occasion. Westin, Sophia and Max scattered.

"Pizza, huh? What're we celebrating?"

"We're celebrating us." Edgard dropped a kiss on Chassie's mouth. "I like bein' home with you guys, but some of what Colby said rang true. We do isolate ourselves out here. One way for people to see us as a normal family, is to do normal family things. Like goin' out for pizza on a Wednesday night."

Trevor came up behind him and wrapped his arms around his waist. "Excellent idea, Ed. where we goin'?"

"The Pizza Barn in Moorcroft." He waited, figuring he hadn't quite pulled off innocence.

Chassie opened her mouth, but closed it. Then her eyes took on a determined glint. "By the look on your face, Edgard Glanzer, I know you're aware that Wednesday night is family church night. so there will be lots of them churchy-type families havin' pizza afterward."

"Good. Then they'll see we're happy with our decision to lead this life, and our children are well adjusted and well loved."

Chassie hugged Edgard and then Trevor. "I'll get my coat and make sure the kids are ready."

"So we're kicking dirt in some faces tonight?"

Edgard shivered at the deep rumble of Trevor's voice flowing over his neck. "No. I'm not suggesting we put on a PDA to show the world we don't care. I want people to understand they're not about to run us off. Especially since I suspect we'll be transferring Westin to school in Sundance. We're here for good."

****

Monday morning Westin was bouncing in his seat. From nerves, or excitement, Chassie didn't know.

She draped her arm over his shoulder. "All that jumping is bound to upset your stomach. Can you take a couple of deep breaths so you don't throw up on your first day?"

He nodded.

Chassie kissed the top of his head. Her eyes met Trevor's in the rearview mirror. She returned his smile.

The closer they got to Sundance Elementary, the more jittery she became. Even when she knew they were doing the right thing, she worried about her son getting lost in the hallways or eating alone or dealing with more bullies.

"Mama. You're squeezing me too tight."

"Sorry. I just love you."

"I know."

The semi-circle drop-off zone in front of the building wasn't jammed with vehicles yet. She craned her neck to see behind them. This traffic wasn't bad at all.

"Chass? Baby, do you see that?" Edgard asked softly.

"What? Where?"

"There. Right in front."

When Chassie peered out the window, her jaw dropped.

Lined up in front of the school, were all her McKay relatives and their spouses. Cord and AJ, Colby and Channing, Colt and India, Cam and Domini, Keely and Jack, Kade and Skylar and Kane and Ginger. The other McKays, ones she wasn't related to, were there also—Quinn and Libby, Ben and Ainsley, Tell and Georgia, and Dalton. Plus, her West cousins, Chet and Remy and Boone.

Approximately ten thousand McKay offspring raced around the adults.

After they exited the car, Westin slipped his hand into hers. "Mama? Why are you crying?"

"Because I'm happy that you get to go to school with all your cousins." She sniffled and leaned her head against Trevor's bicep while Edgard stroked her back.

They faced the McKay throng.

Colby stepped forward. "Surprised to see us?"

"Surprised and grateful. And..." She couldn't finish.

"Kids have enough to deal with without all the B.S. that was goin' on at the other school. That won't happen here. We can pretty much guarantee it."

Colt moved to stand next to Colby. "No one wants to take on the McKays one on one, let alone *all* of us. You guys know you've always had our full support with your lifestyle, we just wanted to make sure everyone in town and everyone whose kids attend this school knew it too."

Chassie didn't bother to stop her tears. She'd always felt like she'd had some support in the McKay family, but nothing on this level.

Boone West crouched in front of Westin. "Know what? I transferred from the school in Moorcroft to this one when I was in third grade."

Westin's eyes lit up with the hero worship he reserved for his older, cooler cousin. "Really?"

"Yep. I promise you're gonna like it a whole lot better."

Chassie couldn't believe her scrawny, sometimes mouthy cousin had turned into such a thoughtful young man. And a good-looking kid to boot.

Boone pushed to his feet and hefted his backpack over his shoulder. "Anyone says anything to you, you let me know, okay?"

"Okay."

"Good. I'll see you on the bus." Boone grinned and Chassie swore the girls walking by actually sighed. The boy was on the road to being a heartbreaker.

Then Boone offered his hand to Trevor and Edgard. "I'll keep an eye on your son."

"We appreciate it," Trevor said. Then he looked at his longtime friend Colby. "Above and beyond. You don't have any idea how much this means to all of us. Thank you."

"You're welcome."

And as the trio walked their son into school, they understood their rough road had just gotten a little easier.

ALL KNOCKED UP

A Rough Riders novella featuring Keely and Jack Donohue
from *All Jacked Up* and *Slow Ride.*

AUTHOR'S NOTE

Author's note: This story begins two months after the end of Rough Riders book 14—*Gone Country*...

CHAPTER ONE

Keely—seven months pregnant...

Keely West McKay Donohue had this pregnancy thing down pat.

Well, except for the occasional glitches when her heightened emotional state hit overload and she had a teeny, tiny, barely noticeable…episode or two.

Most of those incidents hadn't really been her fault.

Like when the grocery store had run out of her brand of laundry soap *again* and she'd attempted to express her displeasure to the manager. But he'd refused to listen to reason, calling her consumer's request a crazy woman's rant, *puh-lease*—she hadn't even hit rant stage. Then the weasel had barricaded himself in his office, had her escorted from the premises by a pimply fifteen-year-old and banned her from the store for life. Luckily, the other grocery store in town had been much more accommodating. They'd even assigned her a shopping assistant to personally escort her through the store every time she showed up.

And Jack could've prevented the incident last month if he'd just taken her out for finger steaks like she'd asked him to. His refusal to understand the depth of her craving had forced her to cook the yummy bits of breaded and fried steak herself. So, it wasn't completely her fault that she'd accidentally started a small grease fire in the kitchen and she'd had to call the fire department. The fire department in turn had called the local ambulance crew, and they had contacted her brother Cam—a Crook County Deputy—who had called her entire family. Except no one had remembered to call her husband. So when Jack had come home after work to see the driveway filled with emergency vehicles and McKays, he'd lost his mind.

She'd had to spray him down with the hose to cool him off. Then she'd really caught hell for ruining his bajillion-dollar, triple-worsted wool suit crafted out of special sheep butt hairs or some such. And people claimed she was on edge during this pregnancy?

Besides, Jack had it easy. His job as her baby daddy entailed three things:

1) Sucking it up and listening to her every pregnancy complaint like she was reciting secret stock tips.

2) Keeping her fed and never ever *ever* mentioning the amount of food she consumed on a daily basis.

3) Fulfilling her sexual needs whenever and wherever she wanted; or keeping his dick far away from her on those bad pregnancy days she suspected she'd chop it off if he showed it to her.

Happily those days were mostly behind them now.

Not such a hard list. So why was he dragging his loafers on getting on with checking off task number three today?

Keely had even given him a choice on where he could perform his husbandly duties. While she waited for him to choose, she studied her hot hunk of manflesh. The man defined sexy—who could blame her for wanting to jump his bones all the damn time? His dark hair was disheveled from constantly running his fingers through it. His silk paisley tie remained neatly knotted and he hadn't taken off his suit jacket, which in her mind meant he hadn't really started to work yet. So this was the perfect time for a break. Besides, Jack never really meant *no*.

"Come on, Jack."

"No."

"I'll make it worth your while," she said, adding a purring *rowr*.

"That's what I'm afraid of," Jack said, without looking away from his computer screen. "And stop staring at my crotch to see if I'm getting hard," he warned her.

"Just tell me if your boxers are getting tight?"

"No."

"Why not?"

"Because A, I'm thinking about work not sex, and if you want to see me before midnight, which isn't likely, you'll find a way to entertain yourself and let me finish this. B, if I do take your offer to bend you over the conference table and fuck you until you scream, guaranteed one of your ten billion family members will decide to pop in and interrupt us. *Again.*"

Keely crossed her arms over her chest trying not to feel self-conscious. She could almost rest them on her protruding belly. "That was not my fault. I cannot control my family, Jack."

"I know that only too well," he muttered. "Besides, don't you have a client scheduled?"

"She had to cancel." That's when she knew she should've lied. He'd see her offer as a way to kill time. When in actuality, she saw it as a chance to revisit their spontaneous pre-pregnancy trysts for the first time in what seemed like weeks.

Jack stopped typing and looked at her sharply. "Just because you're bored doesn't mean I am."

Bored? Fuck that and fuck you too, buddy. Or better yet, I wouldn't fuck you right now if you begged me. In fact... Then just like that surly girl disappeared and weepy woman took her place.

Awesome. She hadn't run this hot and cold even as a teenager. She hated that a curt word or a scowl from him set her off into a fit of rage or a river of tears. Yet she was sick of him and everyone else muttering about her out-of-whack hormones.

So she opted to take the high road for a change. "Sorry to interrupt you." Keely pushed off the doorframe and pulled the door shut behind her. Not slamming it. Point for her.

But Jack didn't chase her down.

That thought caused a pang of sadness. But it also steeled her determination to do something besides wait around for him.

Keely grabbed her things from her office. Although it was only three-thirty, she shut off the lights and locked the building.

Once she was in her Escalade tooling down the road, she realized she didn't want to go home. As social as her life was living amongst her assorted McKay and West relatives, she didn't want to hang out with any of them. The baby performed a kick/karate chop maneuver and she rubbed a hand over her belly. "Guess you're fine with it bein' you and me, huh baby D? What should we do? Daddy forbids horseback riding. No more putzing around on the ATV either."

She could go to Ziggy's—see who was celebrating an early happy hour. Throw some darts. Play some pool. But then again...her body weight balance had shifted so much in the last few months that she sucked at darts. Her oversized belly made it impossible to lean over a pool table to make a decent shot.

On impulse she drove to Spearfish.

She wandered around Walmart. Annoyed with herself for being lonely but not wanting any company. Wanting this baby out so badly, but scared to death for it to actually come out. Then the baby did a full belly roll inside her that took her breath away, forcing her to rest on a porch swing in the lawn and garden department.

As she rocked, her thoughts wandered to Jack. First time he'd been snappish with her for a while. He'd been solicitous lately—to the point she suspected the man was walking on egg shells around her.

Can you blame him after your meltdown two weeks ago?

That wasn't her fault. The stupid mixer had gotten stuck and sprayed red velvet cake batter everywhere. What woman wouldn't have thrown it off the deck and beat it to smithereens with a sledge hammer?

But Jack didn't think her behavior was normal. He'd locked up all the power tools in the shed and refused to give her a key to the new paddle lock.

So maybe she'd had a few crazy moments. But instead of fighting back, Jack had become gentle with her. Not that she wanted him to be a dick, but he hadn't been acting like the Jack she knew and loved.

"Ma'am? Are you all right?"

Startled out of her brooding, Keely glanced up at the young Walmart employee. "I just felt a little dizzy and needed to sit."

"Okay." His gaze slid to the cart parked alongside the garden hose display. A cart filled with bags of candy and potato chips. Three liters of strawberry soda. A tube of KY. And two containers of Brussels sprouts. "Is that your cart? Because I can take it up to the checkout for you."

She looked him in the eye and lied. "I have no idea whose cart that is. It was there when I sat down."

"Oh. I'll just move it out of your way then."

She sighed. So much for sneaking junk food into the house. But her Gestapo husband would've confiscated it anyway and lectured her on bad eating habits. He found no humor in her pointing out that her cravings weren't clichéd like pickles and ice cream.

So it was the first time she'd ever left Walmart empty-handed.

Hungry—*again*—Keely stopped into a sports bar for a burger and ordered a salad, rather than a mountain of French fries. With her feet up on the bench seat, she watched the news and *Wheel of Fortune*. When she glanced at the clock, she realized she'd managed to kill three hours since she'd left the office.

But she still didn't want to go home.

She checked the newspaper for movie show times. Two movies she'd never convince Jack to see were playing. Perfect way to entertain herself.

In the nearly empty theater she chose a seat where she could put her feet up. By the time the movie ended, her restlessness had abated and even baby D had settled down. So she opted to make it a double feature. For the second movie she armed herself with a jumbo bucket of popcorn slathered with butter, an extra-large box of Sugar Babies and a caffeine-free soda.

Mood lighter after the sappy love story and an action flick where the hero had blown up a shit ton of stuff, she sang along with the country tunes on the radio. So she didn't hear the siren behind her, but she sure noticed the flashing lights in her rearview mirror.

So much for her good mood.

Keely watched as her brother Cam got out of the deputy's car. By the time he reached her she'd rolled the window down. She felt her own panic rise when she saw the panic on his face. "Cam. What's wrong?"

"Jesus Christ, Keely. Are you okay?"

"Yes, I'm okay. Why wouldn't I be?"

"Because Jack's been going out of his goddamned mind the last four hours trying to track you down." He stuck his head in the window. "Where's your cell phone?"

"I don't know. I must've left the house without it. Or left it at the office."

"You are a pregnant woman. You need to have that phone on you at all times, do you hear me?"

Enough. She was too damn old for another ass-chewing session, especially when she had to pee again. "Is that some kind of Crook County law I wasn't aware of, Deputy? Are you gonna write me a fucking ticket for not having my cell phone on my person?"

"Don't be a smart ass."

"Don't be a pain in my ass," she shot back. "And I don't need a goddamn lecture from you—"

"Yes, you do, when your husband has called the entire family to find out where the hell you are! He's worried sick, Keely. Are you really blaming him when you've been out of contact for hours?"

Her mouth dropped open. "Are you kiddin' me? I went to the movies after my husband *told* me to leave him alone so he could work! And then he has the balls to act all concerned, like it's my fault? Bullshit." She glared at Cam. "Not only did the bastard call my family to tattle on me, he called you and put out a BOLO on me too? Un-fucking-believable. He's really gonna wish he hadn't done that when I use a croquet mallet on his goddamned laptop and cell phone." Just thinking about beating the fuck out of his precious electronics made her almost giddy.

Cam retreated from the car window. "Keely. Hon. Just chill out."

"What?"

"The look on your face…"

"Is what?" she demanded.

He blurted, "Really freakin' close to evil," and took two steps back from the door so she couldn't take a swing at him. "Remember. This has all been a misunderstanding. You're safe. That's all that matters. Why don't I call Jack and tell him—"

"You'd be better off calling a fucking ambulance because I'm gonna kick his ass when I get home."

Keely rolled up the window and sped off.

If her brother wanted to give her a speeding ticket, fine. But he could damn well do it in her driveway.

****

Jack paced on the front porch.

When he saw the lights of Keely's car, he could finally breathe. He'd nearly gone bald the last four hours, pulling out his hair, desperately trying not to think of worst-case scenarios.

Cam had warned him Keely was mad—really mad, boiling mad, mad like he'd never seen her. But Jack wasn't worried. Her pregnancy mood swings were so erratic she might be whistling a happy tune after she'd had time to think on the drive home about her inconsiderate behavior. She might even throw herself into his arms with a tearful apology.

He plastered on a smile, prepared to be magnanimous.

But the door to the Escalade was thrown open so hard the metal supports should've bent backward. Her boots hit the pavement before he could offer to help her out. Then she slammed the driver's door with enough force the entire car shook.

But it was nothing compared to how hard Keely shook.

Shit. "Keely—"

"Not a fucking word, Jack-ass. I'm so pissed off at you right now you'd better be glad I actually came home."

He took a step toward her and she growled. His wife actually fucking growled at him.

This was not good.

"Last warning to back off. I've had to pee since I left Spearfish and getting pulled over by my brother has just made it worse...and that's your fault too." She stomped up the stairs.

Undeterred, he followed her. "Do you have any idea—"

Keely whipped around so fast he didn't have time to duck the blow from her purse. A purse she was now swinging around like a mace. He was so shocked at the vicious expression on her face that he didn't manage to dodge the second or third blow.

"Jesus, Keely. Will you knock it off?"

The next time she swung, he grabbed the strap and tugged the pink zebra cowhide bludgeoning tool from her fingers.

"Fine, have it," she yelled. "It wasn't doin' enough damage to you to suit me anyway." She stepped back and braced her hand against the house.

"Come on, Keely. Can we please talk about this?"

"No."

Count to ten. "I'm serious."

"So am I." She jammed her heel into the bootjack and removed her right boot.

"Can you please try and be reasonable?"

"Reasonable?" she repeated. "You wanna talk about bein' reasonable? You're the one who told me to buzz off and leave you alone to work."

"You took that out of context."

"Bullshit." Keely removed her other boot. "You said you wouldn't be home until midnight and I should find something to do to entertain myself."

Had he really said that?

"So are you all fired up because I wasn't standing on the porch holding your pipe and slippers to welcome you home?"

"Like that'd ever happen."

Keely growled at him again.

"Maybe I did mention I might be working late. But that doesn't change the fact that I couldn't get ahold of you when my workday ended."

"Since when am I at your beck and call, Jack Donohue?"

Where the hell had that come from? "You have to admit it's pretty irresponsible for you—a pregnant woman in a rural area—to forget your phone. What if you'd had car trouble?" he demanded.

"Then my brother, who was scouring the county for me, could've given me a ride home since you called the fucking *sheriff's* office like I was a runaway wife. I absolutely cannot believe you'd—"

"Keely. Calm down."

"Calm down?" She reached for her boot. "The fuck I will!"

The first one missed him, but the second boot hit him square in the shin. "Goddammit, that's enough!"

"No it's not! You have no idea how furious I am right now." Keely picked up a potted plant and started toward him. "You humiliated me in front of my whole family, Jack. And no doubt you'll blame this, like you blame everything else, on my out-of-control pregnancy hormones!"

"Trust me, buttercup, this psycho redneck behavior is one hundred percent you, and has nothing to do with the baby—" was all he got out before she hurled the flower pot at his head. "I cannot fucking believe you just did that."

"Then you'd better not come into the kitchen because knives are a lot harder to duck, asswipe." Keely stormed into the house. She slammed the door and he heard the snick of the lock as she locked him out.

Locked out. Of his own goddamned house.

Jack yelled, "Real mature, Keely."

Yeah, real mature yelling at your pregnant wife.

He slumped into the closest chair.

How had this escalated to this point?

You overreacted.

Okay, maybe the call to Cam had been unnecessary. But Keely didn't really believe that he'd called her family to find out where she was as some attempt at humiliation? He'd never do that to her. Jack knew how hard she'd struggled not to be seen as the baby who needed constant supervision and protection. But he'd been frantic because it was so unlike her to be incommunicado for that long. Wanting to know where she was wasn't a control thing. He missed her, and yeah, he'd felt guilty for snapping at her and blowing her off. He'd initially called her to tell her he'd finished work early because he wanted to spend time with her. But it'd turned into full-blown panic at hour three.

All he could do now was give her time to calm down. After being married for almost four years he ought to know a way to fix this.

Grovel.

Like hell. He ought to spank her.

Jack swept up the dirt and broken pot. He dug in her purse for her house keys and ended up finding her cell phone—her completely dead cell phone.

At least she'd had the phone with her.

Like that would matter now.

After he'd let himself inside, he wandered into the kitchen. He washed his hands and face, and eyed the butcher block for missing knives.

Then he wandered through the rest of the main level. Keely wasn't in the bathroom, den, living room, dining room or out on the back deck. He scaled the stairs to the second floor. Not in the nursery. Or the other three bedrooms.

The door at the end of the hallway, which led to their bedroom suite, was shut.

Probably locked.

Too bad. He'd kick the damn door in if he had to.

But it wasn't locked.

Jack stepped inside the moonlit room and froze when he saw Keely standing by the big bay window.

She wore a nearly see-through white cotton nightgown that made her look like a goddess in the moon's silvery glow. The way her dark hair trailed down her back, the swell of her abdomen and the heavier weight of her breasts only added fuel to the fire of lust burning inside him.

That's when he knew what she needed—what they both needed.

He moved in front of her and trapped her gorgeous face in his hands, tilting her head to meet his gaze. Then his mouth crashed down on hers and he kissed her with every ounce of passion and hunger she aroused in him just by existing.

Keely didn't deny his kiss or fight him, except to grab his shirt to pull him closer. They kissed crazily; mouths avid, bodies straining.

Jack herded her toward the bed. He broke the kiss, sliding his mouth to her ear. "Keely. I love you. So goddamned much. And I need you. Now. Like this."

"Yes. God, please."

He lifted the nightgown over her head. He filled his hands with her breasts and teased her neck with open-mouthed kisses and tiny sucking bites.

She arched into him and moaned.

"Sit," he ordered and inserted himself between her thighs. His hands followed the contour of her belly, amazed at how her body grew and changed every day. "So beautiful," he murmured. "Every inch of you."

"Jack, I—"

He took her mouth again.

But sneaky Keely wrested control, her sensual kisses destroying him while she unbuttoned his shirt. Her hands raced over his torso, her fingers digging into his flesh. Then her mouth was on his chest, her tongue flicking his nipples between soft, suctioning kisses.

His blood pounded so hard even his skin throbbed. Her every lick and nibble made him hiss.

Jack grabbed a handful of her hair and tugged her head back. "Behave. My way. Or no way. Understand?"

"Bossy."

He cupped the outer swell of her stomach and started a trail of kisses from her sternum, straight down her belly. Rubbing his razor-stubbled cheek across the roundness until she squirmed. "You are so fucking sexy when you're pregnant." Before she responded, he smooched her belly button and kissed his way down the lower curve of her abdomen, dropping to his knees. He spread her knees wide and jammed his tongue deep into her cunt, filling his mouth, his senses with her essence.

"Jack!"

He lapped at the sweet stickiness, swirling his tongue through her soft tissues. Giving her no respite as he drove her higher and harder with each suck and flicker of his tongue. "Come for me fast, cowgirl. So I can fuck you."

"Then leave your mouth right there," she panted.

Jack tongued her clit relentlessly. When her thighs went rigid, he fastened his mouth to the swollen nub and sucked with enough force his teeth pressed into her quivering flesh.

"Yes. Yes!"

He automatically looked up to watch her as she unraveled, but he couldn't see over the baby bump. No matter. He could feel the strength of her orgasm pulsing against his lips. Those low-pitched groans of pleasure did it for him every fucking time, and his cock jerked against his fly in anticipation.

Keely didn't slump back on the bed and sigh when the last pulse faded. She curled her hands around his face. "You rock at that, GQ."

He dragged an openmouthed kiss from one side of her belly to the other. Keeping his heated gaze on hers, he said, "Stand up."

Soon as they were both upright Jack claimed her mouth again, twisting a handful of her silky hair around his palm. He maneuvered her against the wall. He let his lips drift on the underside of her jaw, stopping at her ear. "I want to fuck you hard. You all right with that?"

She nuzzled his cheek. "I'm always all right with that."

"Turn around and brace yourself."

Keely nipped his jaw hard enough he felt a bite of pain before her saucy, sassy tongue snaked out and soothed the sting. Then she spun around and waggled her ass at him.

Oh, she'd pay for that taunt.

Jack ditched his pants and boxers. Then he swatted her right butt cheek hard, keeping his hand between her shoulder blades when she emitted an indignant yelp. "That one is for whipping your boots at me."

Her butt cheeks clenched; she knew he wasn't done.

Jack smacked her left butt cheek. "That one is for throwing a flower pot at me." Then he slapped both butt cheeks simultaneously, down low, where her ass curved into her thighs. "And that one is because I know how much you love me smacking your ass before I fuck you." He aligned his cock and filled her with one deep thrust.

Keely lifted her head and moaned. "Just like that."

Tempting to deny her and stay balls deep in her tight, wet heat. Barely moving. He could come that way, never pulling out fully. It drove her crazy because it took longer to reach the detonation point, even when the explosion was always worth the wait.

But he wanted it hard, fast and without pause. Needing that adrenaline pumping through his body as he bottomed out in her soft cunt on every deliberate thrust.

He pulled out and rammed into her again. And again. Loving the sensation of her softness cushioning his pistoning hips as he pounded into her over and over.

"God, I missed this."

"Me too." His heart thundered. His pulse throbbed in his ears, his groin and his neck. It'd been ages since they'd gone at it this intensely; he wouldn't be setting endurance records because it felt too goddamn good to stop and savor it. "Keely, I can't—"

"Don't hold off on my account, Jack. I already came once. Even if I don't come again, I love it this way."

His hands gripped her hips as he powered into her. His body urged *faster*. His brain...well, his brain wasn't really functioning beyond convincing him his basic life need at that moment was to come.

Six more rapid strokes and he was there.

"Squeeze around me," he rasped.

Keely bore down with her inner muscles.

His cock jerked, sending blasts of heat against her pussy walls as those muscles clamped down, pulling every bit of seed from his balls. Every bit of reason from his brain.

Every bit of anger and frustration with his wife was gone as well.

Nothing compared to make-up fucking after a big fucking fight. *Nothing.*

He hadn't realized he'd been holding his breath until black spots wavered behind his eyelids and he swayed. He reached for the wall.

"Jack? You okay?"

"No." He laughed. "Sorry that went so fast."

"Mmm. I'm not complaining since I had another O at the end," she purred.

He eased out of her body and curled his hands around her shoulders to lift her away from the wall.

"Thanks. I'm a little off-balance these days. And that's without you fucking me senseless."

He slid his hands down her chest, stopping to caress her breasts before placing his hands on the outer swell of her abdomen. "Keely, I love you. You are my world. I'm sorry you doubted that even for a second today."

Keely leaned back into him. "I don't doubt that. I just miss you. I miss us. I miss us bein' together nekkid and sweaty like this. I miss spending time with you even if we're snuggled up on the couch when you're working on your laptop."

"I know I've been distracted trying to get everything done before baby D's birthday... I miss you too, cowgirl. So please, come to bed with me," he murmured in her hair, his body still quaking from sex that always rocked his world.

"I have to go to the bathroom first." She sighed. "Sorry to dampen the afterglow of hot sex."

Jack chuckled and kissed her temple. "It's okay."

As soon as Keely rolled onto the bed—naked, that was a bonus—Jack pulled her close. "Rest that baby on me for a while." He wedged his right side under her left side, his stomach bearing the weight of hers, nestling her head on his shoulder and tangling their legs together.

Keely sighed.

He lived for that contented sound. He played with her hair, and placed his other hand on her belly. "Baby been active today?"

"Really active practicing martial arts moves with flying elbows and kicking feet. But naturally it's asleep now."

"Did it sleep through...?"

"Us fighting? Or us fucking?"

"Both."

"Slept through both."

"Good." Jack pressed his lips to her forehead. "I'm sorry. About earlier."

"Me too. We haven't had a fight for a while."

He looked down at her with disbelief. "Uh, yeah we have."

"When?"

"Last month? When you took after me with a pitching wedge in the driveway? That wasn't a fight?"

Keely snorted. "No. That was a warning if you left your stupid golf clubs on the front porch again, I'd repurpose them as weapons."

"So noted."

"Might come in handy to use on my brothers. Are they gonna show up tomorrow gunning for me because you called them to tattle I was MIA?"

"No. Jesus. Don't even joke about that. And for the record, I didn't call your whole family. I called Cam and your mom." He groaned. "Except your dad answered the phone and demanded details on *what I'd done to piss off his daughter now.* After nearly four years of marriage I'm still trying to prove I'm good enough for you."

"I'm a daddy's girl, what can I say?" She poked him in the chest and teased, "You'll know what it's like to have a daughter in, oh, roughly two months."

"Wrong answer, cowgirl. We are *only* having boys."

Keely propped her chin on his shoulder and looked at him. "Jack, we haven't even discussed baby names."

"Because we only need one." He grinned. "Jack junior."

"Be serious."

"I am. Our first son will be named Jack Donohue, junior. We can call him JJ."

She rolled her eyes. "And I suppose a girl would be called what...Jackie?"

"Nope." Jack kissed her nose. "Because we're only having sons, remember?"

"Whatever. But no matter the first name, the middle name of every child—boy or girl—will be McKay."

"Your dad will love that."

"I could tell him it was your idea," she cooed with total sarcasm. "That'd earn you some brownie points."

"I am *not* a suck-up. And Carson would just think I was a pussy if I acted like one."

After a while, she said, "We start childbirth classes next month."

Don't groan. "I know."

Keely drew circles on his chest. "Us having a baby hasn't impacted your life much at all, has it? Besides having to deal with your moody pregnant wife."

The odd thing was, he'd thought about this, but they'd never discussed it. "Us having a baby hasn't impacted my life *yet*," he emphasized. "So yes, to some extent, I can forget about it while I go about my daily business. But I never forget it's always there for you. You're the one literally carrying the load, Keely. The baby is changing your body, your moods, determining what you can and can't do. I feel like..." He paused, unsure how she'd take his brutal honesty.

"You can tell me anything, no matter how strange it might be."

"Our baby is some vague concept. I see it moving in you. We've readied the nursery, we've looked at the ultrasound pics, which is just fucking bizarre because they make me afraid we're having an alien."

Keely laughed. "Doesn't look like a human, that's for sure."

"Us being in the family way won't affect me until you go into labor and I know that baby is coming out—one way or another. So I'm in stasis."

"That's how I feel most days too."

The skin beneath his hand rippled and he watched as an elbow or a knee moved along the surface like a shark's fin on the water until it disappeared. "Holy shit. Did you see that?"

"I definitely felt it."

"Does it hurt?"

"A little. Mostly it's just weird having something living inside me." She smiled softly—almost serenely and placed her hand over his on her belly. "But it is really freakin' cool, too."

Jack tucked a hank of hair behind her ear. "That it is."

She yawned. "Sorry."

"I know you're tired. Can you fall asleep like this?" Keely's tendency to snuggle up with him at night had ended the fourth month of her pregnancy. He'd missed her sprawled all over him.

"Uh-huh. But I'll probably wake you when I have to get up in a while and use the bathroom again."

"I won't mind." Jack pulled the covers over them.

"About the flowerpot..."

"No need to apologize. It's over and done with."

"I wasn't gonna apologize. I was gonna remind you to buy me a replacement tomorrow. Since the destruction of the poor pot of *impatiens* was your fault."

He didn't think she'd appreciate the irony that'd she'd angrily hurled a container of *impatiens* at him so he didn't mention it.

CHAPTER TWO

Keely—eight months pregnant...

"Look at all this cute stuff." Keely eyed the baby gifts stacked on the dining room table. "I can't believe how many people showed up."

"Your Aunt Kimi certainly outdid herself on this baby shower. I swear she would've invited everyone in three counties if I hadn't culled her guest list. Were you disappointed that Ramona couldn't be here?"

"No. I'm happy that she's finally got a decent man in her life. Chassie felt bad about missing it too, but both she and baby Isabel have a nasty cold and she didn't want to infect me."

"I know Vi was disappointed Chase and Ava weren't here this weekend with their darling little boy Cooper."

"I understand it's hell taking a baby with an ear infection on a plane— even a private plane."

Keely's mother picked up a plate with remnants of blue and pink frosting on the plastic fork and tossed it in the garbage. "It was sweet of Vi and Rielle to bake the cake."

"I'm a sucker for cake."

"I know you are, sweetie. You crashing from the sugar buzz yet?"

"Maybe. I am tired. I hate bein' so freakin' tired all the time." The ladies who'd attended the shower smirked and said the tired aspect wouldn't go away after the birth—that was the universe's way of preparing her for sleepless nights and the demands of parenting.

A bunch of horseshit, if you asked her. Her tiredness stemmed from carrying around fifty extra pounds.

Keely's mom put an arm around her shoulders, directing her to a recliner in the den. "Put your feet up. Sweetie, you sure you're okay? You look a little...off."

"I am. This is all a lot to process."

"True, but I know that's not what put that wrinkle in your brow. So what's really bothering you?"

Keely knew her mom would see through flippancy or badger her if she hedged, so she admitted, "I'm scared."

"Of?"

"Of everything having to do with having a baby. I've been hearing childbirth horror stories and—"

"Keely West McKay." Her mother sat on the ottoman and set her hand on Keely's knee. "You have to stop listening to them."

"But it seemed everyone wanted to share theirs with me today. I've heard about back labor, and all the different tears, rips and fissures that can happen to and around my va-jay-jay. Not to mention the discussions of cracked and bleeding nipples, sleep deprivation, months of postpartum depression and the death knell of my sex life."

"Oh pooh. Scare tactics. Those women only wanted to prove their expertise, for lack of a better term, in something they've experienced. Plus, there is competition about who has the most horrifying childbirth story. I swear I heard that friend of yours from high school, Mary what's-her-name, talking about her episiotomy. There's not that much skin down there to sustain the two hundred stitches it took to sew her up." Her mom sighed. "Okay, she didn't actually say two hundred stitches, but she made it sound that bad to scare you."

"Were you worried when you were pregnant with Cord?"

"Terrified. I was twenty years old and my mother had died the year before so I had no one to talk to who'd been through it. Then again, in those days, the details of childbirth weren't discussed. So it is good that attitude has changed and women are comfortable sharing their stories. And back then, men weren't expected to be in the delivery room."

Keely frowned. "Daddy cooled his boots in the waiting room while you labored alone?"

She shook her head. "They tried to keep him out, but your father"—she smiled—"defines stubborn. He told the hospital staff he didn't abandon his heifers when they were birthing their first calves and he damn well wasn't going to abandon his wife."

"Omigod. A cattle analogy when you were in labor? Really?"

"Yes, which just proves he is a cattleman to the core," she said dryly. "But Carson was such a rock through all the deliveries. He never left my side." She laughed. "But I swear, the man looked ready to faint when the doctor lifted you up and said, *it's a girl.*"

"Daddy didn't always know what to do with me, huh?"

"Then or now." Keely's mom squeezed her hand. "We've been blessed with twenty-six grandchildren. Most days I can't wrap my head around that number. Your father never worried when any of his daughters-in-law were expecting. Although we were both devastated for Colby and Channing when she lost the baby. But he's worried about you."

Surprised, Keely blurted, "But why?"

"He was the same way with me, with every pregnancy. Mentioning that women still died in childbirth—even in modern times."

"Daddy *said* that to you?"

"No. He said it to Cal and Kimi told me. So I cut the man some slack when he wanted to fuss over me when I was pregnant. And he's mentioned that same concern about you to me a time or two. Parental worry never goes away. Even when you're a grown woman with a family of your own. Your father loves all you kids. But sweetheart, you are something special in his world."

"Ma. You're gonna make me cry."

She leaned over and kissed Keely's forehead. "We love you, sweetheart. And we couldn't be happier for you and Jack."

"I'm still scared."

"I know. Just count yourself lucky that Jack will be involved in all aspects of raising your child. Your dad never changed a diaper. Not one."

Keely could not wrap her head around that. All of her brothers and male cousins had no issue with diaper duty. "Didn't you tell Daddy tough shit and suck it up?"

"We fought about it, trust me. I argued that he had no issue sticking his entire arm up a cow's rectum and being covered—and I mean covered—in cow shit on a daily basis, but he gagged at the thought of one poopy baby diaper." She rolled her eyes. "That was his generation. Be thankful Jack is of another generation."

The front door opened and Jack and his mother entered the dining room, deep in conversation. Keely's eyes narrowed. Correction. It appeared sweet Doro Donohue was ripping her son a new one.

"You're back just in time, daddy-to-be," Carolyn trilled. "There's a ton of stuff to be hauled upstairs to the nursery."

Jack flashed Carolyn a smile. "I'm sure Keely will want to show me everything before I become her pack mule." He crossed the room and swept his hand over her belly as he kissed her. "You okay?"

"My ankles are swollen. And I'm tired."

"Probably from a sugar buzz. How many pieces of cake did you eat?"

"One."

"And how many pieces did you sneak in the kitchen?"

She swatted at him. "None of your business. Why?"

"Because you have a dab of frosting right here." He licked the corner of her mouth. "Mmm. Sugary-sweet and tastes like guilt."

"Hey, the baby likes cake."

"I think *my* baby likes cake." He murmured, "You know, we haven't used frosting as body paint in a while."

A throat cleared behind them and they both turned.

"Since you've had people in your house all day, I'm sure you two would like alone time." Keely's mom had moved to stand by Doro. "We'll get out of your hair."

"Ready to go whenever you are," Doro said.

Jack frowned. "Where are you going?"

"Out to celebrate with Carolyn, Kimi and Vi."

"Since Joan came to the shower she's going out with us too," Carolyn added. "Don't worry. We've lined up designated drivers to pick us up at the Golden Boot if things get out of hand."

"What?" Keely and Jack said simultaneously. Then Jack demanded, "Carolyn, are you seriously taking my mother out drinking?"

"Oh, pooh. Don't look so shocked. This is a rite of passage for your mom; a woman becoming a grandmother for the first time. Who better to initiate Doro into that world than the McKays?"

"She has a point, Jack," Keely said with a laugh.

"Don't encourage her, Keely."

"I don't need your permission to not act my age, Jack Donohue." Doro straightened her shoulders. "And I say don't wait up for me either."

The last thing Keely heard was Jack's mom asking if Carolyn knew any single men.

"Now I need a damn drink," Jack grumbled, walking to the bar to pour himself a Scotch.

Keely followed and hoisted herself onto a bar stool. "Looked like you and your mom were having an argument when you walked in."

"We were." Jack uncapped the crystal decanter and poured. "Seemed her sudden need for a trip to the store to buy antacids was a trick to have a private conversation with me about my business trip tomorrow."

Keely glanced down at her hands.

Then Jack's fingers were beneath her chin, forcing her to look at him. "You told me you were okay with this trip, buttercup."

"I am. Or I'm not, depending on the hour."

He waited, those mesmerizing green eyes both patient and concerned.

"I know it's an important job. I know you're only going now so you won't have to go in the next three months. I know it's only a week. I know I'm still three weeks from my due date."

"You know all that, but...?"

"But there's part of me that doesn't want you to go. And no, I wasn't complaining to your mother about it. I didn't even mention it. What did she say?"

"That I'd better not be putting work ahead of my family. My dad did that and landed himself in an early grave because of it." His jaw tightened. "Like I needed that fucking reminder, along with all the other things that are running around in my brain."

"What kinds of things?"

He drained his drink. "Too much guilt and bullshit male stuff that'd make you roll your eyes and wonder if you married a man or a whiny pussy."

Keely slid off the stool and cut around the end of the bar to hug him—as much as she could with beach ball baby between them. "I know you're a man. All man. So since we're alone, maybe you oughta prove that to me a couple of times before you leave."

Jack smoothed her hair away from her cheek. "You really up for this, cowgirl? It's been a long day. You said your ankles are swollen."

"Then how's about if you make my pussy swollen, so I really have something interesting to bitch about at the breakfast table tomorrow morning."

"God, I love you."

"Well, I *am* unbelievably charming and sexy as hell." Keely kissed him and tugged his bottom lip between her teeth, just to see that spark of desire flare in his eyes. "We better do it all we can in the next three weeks, because it'll be at least six weeks after baby D's birth before we can have sex again."

"Does that ban on sex include anal?" he asked.

"You are such a guy."

He shrugged. "Just being practical."

"Come on. Let's do it on the recliner. I'll even bring a piece of cake so you can lick frosting off my nipples."

****

One week later...

Keely prided herself on providing a full twenty minutes of random conversation before grilling her cousin Dalton about his love life. "So what's this I hear about you and Addie Voorhees dating?"

Dalton shrugged. "We're spending time together. I've known her forever. She's sweet."

"That she is. But isn't she—"

"Please don't say that you're surprised because she's a nice girl and totally not my type."

"Wow. Defensive much? That wasn't what I was gonna say."

"Shit. Sorry. I've just heard that a lot. From everyone in town. Including several members of our family." Dalton cocked his head and offered the dimpled grin that'd been causing him problems his entire life. "So what were you gonna ask?"

Now that Keely thought about it...this question would probably get his back up even more. "Just that Addie and Rory Wetzler are best friends, right?"

"They were inseparable during high school. But Rory's been living in Laramie for the past six years. Why?"

Keely shrugged and swigged her soda.

"You oughta just spit out whatever's put that cat-stealing-cream look on your face, Keely," he drawled.

"Fine. I just find it...odd, that you and Addie started seeing each other a couple months after Rory went to study in South America."

Dalton's eyes narrowed. "Why's that odd?"

Because I don't think Rory would be okay with Addie dating you. Although Keely prided herself on honesty, this was one time where she'd hedge. "Didn't you and Rory have a thing?"

He squirmed. Her big, bad, brawling baby cousin blushed beet red. "We're friends. Or we were friends."

"What happened? Because Rory caught the bouquet at our wedding and everyone said you two were all kinds of cozied up on the dance floor after that."

"That was almost four years ago," he pointed out. "A lot can change."

"I guess. Sierra told me Rory took a swing at you in the bar last fall before Christmas. She didn't say why."

"There's a first," he grumbled. "Look, it's complicated, okay? And why do you care? It's not like Rory is even around now. Addie said Rory didn't take issue with it when she told Rory that me'n her were dating."

Bullshit. "You're probably right. Pay no attention to me. I dated Jack's brother before we got married. Jessie was married to your brother Luke before she and Brandt got hitched, so I guess it's not that odd."

"And...there it is. Another McKay family member hearing wedding bells in the distance for me long before I hear them," Dalton said dryly.

Keely laughed. "Guilty. Let's change the subject. So how'd you get roped into Keely duty?"

Dalton lifted a brow and repeated, "Keely duty?"

"Your poker face is for shit, Dalton McKay. For the past week since Jack has been gone, everyone in the McKay family and their dog—literally—has stopped by to check on me. Like I'll have a nervous fucking breakdown if I have to spend time alone. I have two weeks left until my due date. If this baby takes after its father, it'll be late anyway."

"Well, I musta missed the McKay family memo about my rotation on babysitting bratty you. I stopped by to talk to Jack. Had no idea he was gone."

"Oh." Since when was he buddy-buddy with Jack?

He grinned. "No retort on the *bratty you* comment?"

"I was practicing bein' mature and ignoring it."

"With that..." Dalton stood. "Need me to do anything before I go?"

Keely shook her head. "I'm fine." She heaved herself out of the chair. "My butt's asleep so I'll walk you out."

A blast of heat hit her as soon as she stepped onto the front porch. The temp had hit one hundred degrees the last three days. Being nine months pregnant was miserable. Add in the August heat and, well, she had no idea how pregnant women survived before air conditioning. "Should I tell Jack you stopped by?"

"Nope. I'll catch him some other time."

Which meant Dalton *had* been tasked to keep her company for a few hours. Her youngest cousin had a better poker face than she'd given him credit for.

****

When Keely got up at three a.m. to go to the bathroom for the two hundredth time, she had heartburn so bad she decided to try and sleep upright in the recliner in the den. But the fabric made her sweat. Even the crotch of her pajamas were wet. She shifted her hips and a trickle of water further dampened her panties.

Great. Now I'm peeing my pants?

The tears she'd held in all day poured out. She blubbered as she changed clothes—but her sweat pants wouldn't stay up. She'd stretched the drawstring to the limit around her gigantic belly. So she sat on the edge of her bed, in her underwear, and cried.

Suck it up, buttercup. Won't be much longer and you'll forget all this as you're holding our baby.

Jack's voice in her head snapped her out of it.

She rubbed her belly. "I'm missing your daddy something fierce. I lied when I said I'd be okay if he took this business trip. But he promised it's the last one until you make your appearance. Which I'm hoping is soon."

When Keely stood, liquid trickled down her leg. A lot of liquid.

She froze.

She wasn't peeing herself; her water had broken.

"No." This couldn't be happening. She hadn't meant she wanted the baby out this soon! Jack wasn't here. She couldn't have the baby without him. He wasn't supposed to be here until late tomorrow night. Or wait. Was that tonight? She glanced at the clock. Four-thirty a.m.

Jack's last big meeting was in four hours.

She mostly stayed out of his business, but he might throw a shit fit if she interrupted him, so she wouldn't call him. He'd call her after he closed the deal anyway.

Okay. She'd just...kill time for a few hours. Watch TV. No big deal. First babies took forever. At least twenty-four to thirty hours, according to all the childbirth books she'd read.

To take her mind off everything, she stripped the bedding and tossed it in the washer.

Good. That'd killed ten minutes.

She ate a few bowls of chocolate-frosted flakes.

Then she stretched out in the recliner with the TV on. She dozed off only to be awakened by a god-awful tightening in her mid-section.

Holy fuck. Was that a labor pain?

Nah. She probably shouldn't have eaten half a box of cereal. And four pieces of toast. And a couple frozen waffles.

Since the sun was up, Keely ventured outside and watered the flowers on the back deck. And the ones on the front deck. By the time she finished, the cramping in her abdomen was getting worse. *Motherfucking hell, that motherfucking hurt.* Then more liquid gushed out.

She needed to go to the hospital now.

She walked inside, grabbed her keys, walked back out and climbed in her car.

****

Jack's phone buzzed at nine-thirty, right after he'd finished his meeting. He looked at the caller ID and his entire body stilled. "AJ? What's going on?"

"Keely's water broke."

His heart rate spiked. "When? Why didn't she call me?"

"Ah, that's the thing. Hang on." He couldn't make out any words from the muffled voices in the background. "Sorry about that. Look, no one knows what's goin' on with her. She drove herself to the hospital this morning without her purse, without her hospital bag, without anything except her keys."

"Jesus. Is she okay?"

"No. She also showed up barefoot, in her pajamas. So, we, ah, think she's in some kind of shock, denial thing since you're not here. Doc Monroe did get her admitted into a private room, but she's refusing to see anyone."

"Even you?"

"Even me."

Christ. He'd felt somewhat justified leaving her because she had so many family members willing to step in. Now when she needed them she was shutting them out?

"I did manage to talk to her for a minute before she called the nurse to have security remove me from her room."

"What did she say?"

"That the two of you decided there'd be no one in the delivery room with you. Period. She says she's sticking to that and waiting for you. When I asked what time you were expected to get to the hospital, she said after your big meeting ended in Arizona. At that point I realized she hadn't even called you yet so I thought I'd better." AJ blew out a frustrated breath. "Look. When does your flight leave?"

"At two. I get into Denver at four...and shit, that won't work. I'll still have to drive another four hours..." He paced, but his mind was not operating on all cylinders. Keely would never forgive him if he wasn't there for the birth. Never. And he wouldn't be able to forgive himself either.

"Jack!" AJ said sharply.

"What?"

"What are you gonna do?"

"I'll charter a plane," he said offhandedly. "Now let me talk to my wife."

"I'm not kiddin' when I say she won't let anyone in the room. Just the nurse. Just Doc Monroe and she's gone to the clinic."

"Then tell her I'm on the phone."

AJ groaned. "Carolyn tried that. As soon as Keely found out you weren't on the phone, she threw the phone at the wall and told her mom to get out or else she'd have Cam arrest her for trespassing."

"Why the fuck would you guys lie to her? Why didn't Carolyn call me?"

"I don't know. I'm just the messenger. So my message is to hurry up and get home." AJ hung up.

Jack called Gavin Daniels, Keely's cousin he'd done business with. "Gavin? Jack. Do you have any private aviation contacts in Tucson? Keely's in labor and I need to get home ASAP. Uh-huh. Rapid or Spearfish—preferably Spearfish. That'll be fine. Cost is not an issue. Thanks. I owe you one. I'm on my way to the airport now."

****

He arrived in Spearfish five hours later. Gavin picked him up and didn't make idle chitchat on the way to the hospital, which Jack appreciated.

Jack nearly ran inside the ER doors. At the receptionist's desk, he said, "Keely Donohue. She's in labor."

"And you are?"

"Her husband, Jack Donohue."

The receptionist clicked the keys. "Looks like you're cleared to go in—wow, looks like you're the *only* one cleared to go in. Down the hallway, and take the first right. They'll clear you through from there."

Jack didn't make it past the first reception area before he was surrounded by McKays, who all talked at once. He let loose an ear-piercing whistle—a trick his wife had taught him.

Silence.

"I appreciate you all being here when I couldn't be. But go home. I promise we'll call when we have news."

"Go home?" Carolyn repeated.

"No way," Carson snapped.

The arguing started immediately.

Jack didn't have time for this. He walked to the next receptionist's desk. "I'm Jack—"

"We know who you are. Your wife had been calling from the room every fifteen minutes to ask if you're here yet. It stopped in the last hour, like she'd given up on you."

His stomach knotted.

"She's in room two. The nurse will fill you in."

Jack scrubbed his hands over his face and inhaled a deep breath before he opened the door.

Keely was lying on her side, curled into a ball with her back toward him. The fetal monitoring device positioned at the head of the bed.

He rounded the opposite side of the bed so not to startle her. Her eyes were closed and her face was pinched with pain. "Hey, cowgirl. How you holding up?"

Keely didn't acknowledge him at all.

Was she really that sound asleep?

Jack ran his hand up her arm. "Keely?"

Her eyes opened. "Jack? Is that really you?"

He kissed her forehead. "Yes. I got here as soon as I could."

"I thought maybe you'd changed your mind."

"About what? Being in the delivery room with you?"

"No. About us havin' a baby."

What the hell? "It's a little late to worry about that now, don't you think?"

"No. I can't believe..." She sat up and started to cry. Blubbering so he couldn't understand anything she said.

Then she flopped back into the mattress. Tears flowed down her face and she cried quietly. She wouldn't even look at him.

Fuck. He could handle anything but her tears. He handed her a wad of tissues but she just balled them in her fist and didn't attempt to mop up the waterworks.

Jack stood by the side of her bed, hands in his pockets, absolutely at a loss. He'd never seen Keely listless and weepy. Might make him masochistic, but he wished she'd take a swing at him. Or yell at him. Hell, he'd even be happy if she threw the pitcher of water at his head. "Buttercup. What can I do?"

"Take me home," she whispered. "I don't wanna be here."

"As soon as we have this baby and everyone is all right, I promise I'll take you home."

Keely shook her head. "Can't we just go home and we'll come back and try again tomorrow? The baby isn't supposed to be here for two more weeks. I'm not ready."

"We've got a few hours to get ready."

"I can't do this."

She really was in shock. He'd never seen that before. "You can. You have to."

"You can't make me." She sniffled. "And if you're gonna be like this then I want you out of my room."

"Like hell."

Keely tried to turn away from him and tune him out.

Jack hated to poke the bear, but pissing her off was the fastest way to snap her out of it. He got right in her face. "So how'd you end up breaking your water?"

She blinked at him. "What?"

"I've been gone for a week. What did you do during that time? Were you tearing around on the ATV or out joyriding your horse, trying to get this baby here faster?"

"No!"

"How'd it happen?"

"I was just sitting on the bed and it felt like I kept peeing my pants. Then it just gushed out—"

"So you just...what? Grabbed your keys, left the house barefoot, in your pajamas, without your damn cell phone—again—and just drove yourself to the hospital? Why didn't you at least call your mom? Or AJ? Or one of the two thousand other McKays who always seem to be underfoot—except when you need them."

"I don't know why..." More tears flooded her eyes. "I just wanted you. I wasn't thinking straight."

"Damn right you weren't. When did you intend to call me? Right, how could you have called me without your cell phone? I swear I'm tethering that thing to your wrist from here on out."

A spark of defiance flashed in her eyes. "Try it."

"I live for a challenge. Maybe I'll take your car keys away too, so you'll have to call someone when you need help because you won't be able to go anywhere by yourself."

"You wouldn't dare."

"I'd do it in a fucking heartbeat. Sometimes your independent streak drives me insane."

That got her back up.

Good. He kept hammering at her. "This is our first baby. I know you're freaked out. I am too. Childbirth has come a long way, but there are still dangers—"

"For your information, buster, women have been havin' babies all over the place since the beginning of time. I don't need you to goddamn lecture me on what it takes to have a baby since I'm the one pregnant! You cannot just show up here and take over like you know what's goin' on when you—"

"So I'm just supposed to stand by and watch you fall to pieces? The baby is coming, whether you're ready or not, whether or not you like it. So suck it up and deal with it."

"Why are you bein' such an asshole?"

"Me?" he asked innocently. "I'm never an asshole to you."

She snorted. "That'll be the day. But you have been less assholish the last few weeks. In fact, you've been downright mushy gushy with me lately…" Her eyes narrowed. "Hey. That was a trick, Mr. Know-it-all, storming in here, saying all that bullshit so I'd get mad."

"Listening to you rant is a damn sight better than watching you cry."

Her bottom lip quivered but she firmed it. "I hate you."

"No, buttercup, you love me."

"So? I still wanna punch your smarmy face, jerkwad."

"I know." Jack watched her settle and inhale a deep breath. He fought a grin seeing her hand was still balled into a fist. "But can we get back to the business at hand first?"

"Always business with you, GQ." She eyed his clothing. "I hope you get baby birth junk and goo all over your snappy suit."

"Now that was just plain mean."

"I can start crying again, if you'd rather."

"God no." He reached for her hand. "Are you having contractions?"

"Yes."

"And...?"

"And they're random and they hurt like a motherfucker."

"What can I do?"

"Tell Doc Monroe to get back here and give me a C-section because I don't think I can do this the normal way."

"*We* can do this the normal way."

"There is no *we*. You don't have amniotic fluid gushing out of your dick nor do you have to push something that weighs six pounds through the small hole at the end of your—"

Jack covered her mouth with his. Then he eased back to stare into her wild eyes. "Yes, *we*. Always *we*, Keely. Always."

"I'm scared," she said in a small voice that ripped at him.

"Me too."

"Oh God, here comes another one."

His mind went blank momentarily at seeing her face twist into a mask of pain. Then something clicked and he remembered what he was supposed to do. "Come on, breathe with me."

Her eyes locked onto his as he led her through the worst of it. Then she slumped against him, burying her face in his neck. "I'm so glad you're here. I can't do this without you."

Jack kissed the top of her head. "Every minute it took me to get here was pure torture."

Doc Monroe came into the room. "Jack, glad to see you made it." She snapped on protective gloves and sat on a small rolling stool at the end of the bed. "Let's see where we are."

The nurse said, "Keely, you need to scoot down so the doctor can check you."

Keely didn't snap off a snarky comment, which was unlike her, especially since she was friends with the doctor. She clutched Jack's hand as she wiggled into position.

Jack never took his eyes off Keely as Doc Monroe examined her.

"Well, you've only dilated another centimeter since my last check. Since it's been fourteen hours since your water broke, and you're not progressing, we'll need to put you on Pitocin to move the labor along." She spoke to the nurse, who nodded as she jotted down the details.

Doc Monroe stood and removed the gloves. "How you holding up, Keely?"

"Better now that Jack is here."

"I figured as much." She eyed Jack—probably so see if Keely's verbal lashing had left physical marks. "Thought you'd be in the doghouse for a lot longer, to be honest."

"The day isn't over yet," Keely retorted.

She laughed. "Okay, Daddy, here's the deal. You are gonna do whatever Keely wants, needs, asks for, to get her through the next couple of hours."

"Hours?"

"Yes, hours. Keely has a ways to go before she's ready to deliver. Pitocin will create stronger, more consistent contractions. I'll be back in a few hours to check on her."

"Don't I need to change into scrubs or something?"

"Not until we're close to the finish line." The doctor spoke to the nurse and they wheeled the IV over.

After starting the IV drip, another contraction hit.

The nurse brought Jack a chair. "Sit. Get comfy. You'll be here a while. If you need anything, hit the call button."

****

Another seven hours passed and Jack was wrung out.

Keely, his beautiful, wonderful, tough cowgirl held it together. She hadn't taken a swing at him, like her brothers had warned him she'd do. She hadn't tried to twist his dick off or knee him in the family jewels, like her brothers had warned him she might try. Good thing, he'd left his cup at home. She'd only called him fuckface-asshatsonuvabitching-goddamn bastard, twice—pretty much a normal day for them.

The harder the contractions, the quieter she became. When the contractions seemed to come without pause, she breathed through every one, keeping a death grip on his hand. Focused on him, she connected so intimately to him he swore he felt her labor pain several times.

Jack fed her ice chips and wiped her face with cool cloths. He rubbed her back. He offered her lots of praise. He did everything he was supposed to do but none of it seemed enough as she struggled to bring their child into the world.

"Jack," Keely panted.

"Yes, sweetheart, what do you need?"

"You should say that to me all the time. Oh God-oh God-oh God— that fucking *hurts!*"

"Look at me."

She shook her head and kept her eyes closed. "Get the nurse. I need to push. I need to push *now.*"

He hit the call button.

The nurse checked her and gave them the thumbs up. "She's at nine." She tossed him a set of scrubs. "I'll stay with her while you change."

Everything in the next fifteen minutes passed in a blur.

Keely had gone into a trance-like state as she faced the final hurdle. He stayed by her side, but he wasn't sure if she knew he was there.

Medical personnel came in and out of the room.

Finally Doc Monroe returned. "Okay, Keely, let's do this thing. Keep focused on your breathing. There are times I'll want you to push and times I won't. Listen to Jack. He'll help you through it."

"Oh God, it fucking burns so bad I need to push," Keely shouted.

"All right, gimme a push."

Jack had to grit his teeth at the painful sound coming from his wife. He didn't know if he'd survive this. He didn't know how he could ever ask this of her again.

"Hold on one second sweetie and breathe. Jack, get her a little more upright and hold on to her."

He tilted the bed and grasped her shoulders.

"Okay, Keely, go ahead and push again," Doc Monroe said.

Keely made a grunting cry. Once. Twice. Then she slumped against him. "I can't."

"You can," he assured her. "We're almost there. I promise."

"Just two more pushes, Keely, and your baby will be here."

He felt Keely gather herself. Then she bore down so hard her entire body shook.

"Hold one second. Good. All right. One more."

Keely reached for his forearm. "Jack—"

"I gotcha. Squeeze me as hard as you need to."

She emitted a triumphant cry and nearly broke his forearm, but he didn't care because he knew she'd done it.

He peered down her body but couldn't see anything.

Doc Monroe laughed. "Congratulations, Donohues, you have a baby girl."

Jack was stunned. If he hadn't been holding on to Keely he might've crashed right to the floor.

A girl?

What the hell did he know about little girls?

Then the bloody, slippery thing was laid on Keely's stomach.

They both just stared at her.

"Omigod. There she is," Keely said in awe. "She's real. She's...ours." She turned her head into Jack's bicep and started to cry.

Jack pressed his cheek into the top of Keely's head, so overwhelmed he couldn't speak.

"Daddy, do you want to cut the cord so we can get her cleaned up and checked out?"

"Ah, sure." But as he reached for surgical instrument, his hand shook so violently he almost dropped it.

Doc Monroe patted his arm. "It's okay. I've got it."

Snip.

Then the nurses whisked the baby away.

She screamed bloody murder.

Jack wanted to go see what they'd done to her to make her cry like that. That wasn't natural...was it?

"Jack?"

"What?"

"You can let go of my shoulders."

"Oh. Sorry."

Keely leaned back into the mattress. Jack kissed her forehead. Her temple and finally her lips. "I love you. That was amazing." He kissed her again. "You're amazing."

"Keely, gotta give me one more push."

She wrinkled her nose. "This was the gross part in the books. The placenta." She sat up and pushed.

"All done. No episiotomy. No tears as far as I can tell," Doc Monroe said and stood. She patted Keely's knee. "Good job, Mama. Lemme check on your girl's stats so you can have her."

Keely placed her hand on Jack's cheek and turned his face toward her. "You okay?"

"No." He shook his head to clear it. "A girl."

"You surprised?"

"To say the least. Both our families are male dominant."

"Well that's about to change in our household," Keely said.

"She weighs eight pounds two ounces," Doc Monroe announced. "She's twenty-two inches long. And she..." She laughed. "You'll see." She wandered over with the bundle and stopped at the foot of the bed. "You feeling up to holding her?"

Keely held out her arms. "Gimme."

"We'll give you half an hour in here and then we'll move you into a regular room."

"Can I have some food, too?"

"I'll let them know." The medical personnel vanished.

"Jack, hand me that pillow."

Keely placed the pillow lengthwise on her lap and laid the baby across it. "Let's unwrap our girl and check her out."

As soon as Keely removed the pink hat, Jack said, "Holy shit. She's got red hair. A lot of red hair." He touched her tiny head. "It's so soft."

They looked at her fingers and toes. Poked at her chubby legs. Marveled at her long arms. Studied her perfectly round, perfectly beautiful little face. She'd mellowed out. She let them poke and prod her without fussing at all.

"Well, what do you think?"

"Honestly? I'm speechless. She's...not an alien," Jack said softly. "But she might as well be. She's so little." He stroked her cheek and she turned her head.

Then she opened her eyes.

And Jack Donohue fell completely in love for the second time in his life.

****

Jack wasn't surprised when the nurse told him that Keely's parents had remained in the waiting room.

After getting Keely settled in upstairs, and fed, he tracked them down. "Come and meet your new granddaughter."

Carolyn practically tackle-hugged him.

Carson just grinned.

Keely was propped up in bed, looking exhausted, but absolutely serene. "Hey. I can't believe you guys stayed after the way I acted..."

"Already forgotten, dear." Carolyn patted her shoulder. "So, let's see her."

"This is Piper McKay Donohue." Keely unwrapped the blanket and pushed the hat back.

"Good Lord, that child has red hair. Well that's a first in the McKay family."

Carson peered and the baby and smiled. "Hey, girlie. I hope that red hair means you're gonna be a feisty hellion who gives your mama as much trouble as she gave me."

"Daddy!"

"She is a beauty," he said softly. "Like her mama. And her grandmamma."

Keely teared up but she held it together.

"There ain't pictures of my mom around, but she was a natural redhead," Carson offered.

Jack kissed his daughter's head and pulled the hat back down. "When I called my mom, she said her mother was a redhead."

"After all the dark-haired babies born into this family...leave it to Keely to do something different."

It'd been a long day for everyone, so Carson and Carolyn stayed about ten minutes.

Jack walked them to the elevator.

Before Carson got in, he clapped Jack on the back and choked out, "Now, son, you'll know."

"Know what?"

"Why I am the way I am about my daughter. Now you'll know what it's like to have a baby girl who lights up your entire world."

The doors closed, leaving Jack feeling like he and Carson McKay had finally found common ground after all.

Chapter Three

Two months later...

"Keely, I think she's hungry."

"Again?" Keely put the lid on the potatoes and walked over to where Jack stood, holding Piper. The man was always holding Piper. If he was home, their daughter was in his arms. He was a doting father absolutely smitten with their child. They both were just giddy about their girl.

They'd adjusted to parenthood much quicker than expected. Mostly because Piper was a ridiculously good baby. She slept for a few hours at a time and only had one fussy night feeding. And Jack insisted on handling that one.

Keely peered at Piper's face as she wiggled and made snuffling, working-up-to-a-big-cry noises. She stroked her chubby cheek. Immediately Piper turned and rooted around looking for food. "Poor starving girl."

"Get settled. I'll bring her to you."

She planted herself in the middle of the couch and lifted her shirt. She hadn't been sure how she'd do nursing, but so far so good. And her boobs were huge, which caused more discomfort, and less *look at my huge hooters!* pride than she'd imagined.

Jack handed Piper off to her, but sat on Keely's left side, snuggled close to watch their baby feed.

Keely breathed a sigh of relief as the tiny mouth latched onto the nipple and her milk let down.

"I can't believe how big she's getting."

"Gavin said she'll be asking for the car keys before we know it."

He shuddered. "I can't even imagine. Let's enjoy every second of her being entirely helpless."

****

Later that night, after Piper had been tucked into her bassinet, Keely lingered in the bathroom, psyching herself up.

So they hadn't had sex in eight weeks. Getting back into the swing of it shouldn't be hard, right?

Keely's image in the bathroom mirror didn't answer her.

She sucked in her stomach, but the pouch of fat didn't budge. But if she was lying down, then her stomach would look flat. Maybe even sort of close to her pre-pregnancy size.

She fluffed her hair into the just-tumbled-out-of-bed style Jack loved. Although lingerie would hide the curvier aspect to her ass and hips, getting it on was too much trouble. Her husband tore the lace and satin off her in record time anyway.

Hand on hip, she practiced a "come and get it" smile. Then she opened the door and sauntered into the bedroom.

Jack sat on the edge of the bed. Her gaze tracked his body. He had the sexiest back. Wide shoulders, rippling muscles tapering into a narrow waist. He'd maintained his drool-inducing physique with the same rigorous attention to fitness as he gave to his business.

So what will he think of her extra softness?

Call it what it is, Keely. Not extra softness. Extra pounds.

Man, her body image was for shit today. Maybe this wasn't the best idea.

But when Jack glanced over his shoulder at her, gifting her with his sexy grin, she was pretty much toast.

She crawled onto the bed and followed the curve of his spine with just one finger. She spread her hands over his back, from the bottom of his shoulder blades to the top.

"What are you up to, wife?"

Her damp lips touched his right ear. "Just admiring the view." She let her mouth connect with his nape as her arms twined around his torso.

Jack released a soft groan when her thumbs brushed over his nipples. "I love that noise," she murmured. "I love touching you like this."

He hissed when she sank her teeth into the arch of his neck.

"I want you, Jack." Her hands slid down the front of his body to the drawstring on his sweatpants. "I want you in my mouth before you pin me to the mattress and fuck me."

"The doctor gave you the green light?"

"Uh-huh." Keely blew in his ear. "Last week. But we've been so baby preoccupied or tired, or the timing has been off." She tugged on his earlobe. "So are we in synch tonight?"

"Perfect synch."

"Good. Crawl up here and lemme put a smile on your face."

Jack kissed the tips of her fingers before disentangling her arms. Then he stood and ditched his sweatpants. Not a shock he'd gone commando. She allowed a smug smile she'd already gotten him hard.

He cupped her face in his hands and kissed her. Not the sweet, lazy kisses they'd shared over the past two months, but a white-hot explosion of passion. Keely had to wrap her hands around his wrists to keep from toppling over backward.

"Maybe I want you on your knees in front of me," he said against her lips.

"My idea. I get to be in charge. Besides, do you really care what position I'm in as long as my mouth is around your cock?"

He laughed softly and pulled away. He stretched out on the bed, spreading his legs and resting his hands behind his head like he was watching TV.

"Is this a challenge?" She scooted between his thighs and let her hair swing across his groin, bracing her hands by his hips. "Because I'm up for it."

"I know you are, cowgirl."

Her wet tongue followed the rim of his cockhead, stopping only to flick the sweet spot. Or to go round and round the engorged tip until his belly muscles quivered.

Keeping her eyes on his, she parted her lips, opened her throat and swallowed him.

"Jesus."

She intended to work him with her mouth. Tease and retreat. Build him up and back off. So when he couldn't take it anymore, he'd take her. Face to face. Basic boring, missionary style sex. But missionary position was anything but boring with Jack Donohue. It'd been six long months since they'd been able to do it that way. And she couldn't wait to be pressed beneath the weight of his body and look into his eyes while he made her come undone.

But first she tortured him. Using every trick she'd ever learned with her teeth, her lips, and her tongue to keep him on edge.

Heady stuff, hearing him groan. Feeling his hips buck up. Knowing he clenched his ass cheeks to try and retain some control. Her oral worship of his cock made her equally squirmy. Her skin tingled from her scalp to her toes. Her pussy was drenched.

"Keely. You're killing me here. I can't hold off."

Those were the magic words. She raised her head and trailed her hair up his torso as she levered her body over his.

The next thing she knew she'd been flipped on her back and Jack hung above her. "As much as I love seeing my come on your face, I much prefer the look on your face when I do this." He plunged into her to the hilt.

Keely arched hard. "Yes. More like that. A lot more."

Jack pressed a kiss on her collarbone. "Can't. Gotta slow it down." He rolled his hips. A steady slide in; a leisurely retreat out.

She drummed her heels on his ass. "Jack. Go faster."

"No."

Her fingers mapped the muscles in his arms. The smooth arc of his shoulders. The strong line of his jaw. "You're so pretty, GQ."

"I'm not fucking pretty," he half-snarled.

"So very pretty," she whispered in his ear. Her mouth followed the corded tendon in his neck, loving the taste of him on her tongue.

Jack kissed her in that bone-melting way of his, giving her that fluttery feeling in her belly. She thought for sure her "pretty" comment would have him all fired up to prove his rougher side.

Wait...was there another reason he kept the pace so slow besides his need to constantly prove his "me man, me satisfy my woman" mantra? Could there be a...physical difference for him?

"How does it feel?" she panted against his throat.

"Amazing."

"Any different? Looser or whatever?"

Jack pulled back and looked down at her. "Feels like I'm making love to my wife after a long stretch of *not* making love to my wife." He threaded his fingers through hers and pinned her arms above her head on the mattress. "Watch my face." His hips began to move again, more forcefully as his cock shuttled in and out of her.

She could never get tired of looking at him. This stunning man who was perfect inside and out. Perfect because he got her.

"What's wrong?"

"Not a damn thing. Just thinking that I missed seeing you like this, moving above me."

"I missed it too. And you're about to get your request for me to move faster."

"Yes."

He pulled out completely and thrust in fully on every stroke. It was glorious reminder how in tune they were with each other. Such a secret thrill to realize having a baby hadn't changed this between them.

Her breath caught. So close.

"Come on, buttercup. Take me with you."

The instant she felt the tingling in her groin, signaling her orgasm was about to start, she felt the other tingling sensation in her breasts. The one indicating that her milk was about to let down.

No. Not now.

Jack had switched into a pushup position, his pelvis grinding against her clit on every thrust, knowing that set her off.

But instead of an outstanding orgasm, Keely watched in silent horror as milk shot out of her nipples and coated Jack's chest. Milk dripped back onto her even as more milk squirted out.

He stopped moving.

She'd immediately clapped her palms over her breasts to try and stop the spray.

Omigod omigod omigod this can't be happening repeated on a loop in her brain. Her entire body flushed with mortification. "Get off me."

"What?"

"I said get off me right now!" She shoved him at him.

Jack pushed upright. "Keely? What's—"

She rolled off the bed and ran into the bathroom, slamming the door behind her.

Locking the door behind her.

Keely stepped into the shower and cranked it on cold, standing under the spray despite her chattering teeth, hoping the shock of icy water would shut down her milk ducts.

Don't you mean your udders?

Some days she felt like nothing but a milk machine. And she really had become one tonight. A faulty one, spewing milk all over her husband. While they'd finally been...

She shuffled away from the streaming water, pressed her forehead to the shower wall and sobbed.

Was this really how it'd go? She couldn't even have sex with her husband because if she orgasmed she'd do her Bessie the milk cow imitation all over him?

Despite the frigid temp of the shower, her cheeks still burned with shame.

Would Jack look at her breasts warily? Would he even touch them again?

She cried harder. Feeling such a sense of loss.

The water shut off.

"Keely—"

"I locked the goddamned door for a reason, Jack. Go away."

"No." His warm body covered hers. "At first I thought I'd hurt you when I'd picked up the pace."

She shook her head. Made her feel even worse that he thought he'd hurt her and she'd just left him there.

"I'm not going anywhere. So if you want to stand here naked in the shower all night, that's what we'll do."

She hunched her back away from him.

His mouth skated along the slope of her shoulder. "But I'd really like to finish what we started."

"I already gave you one milk bath," she snapped. "You wanna go for two?"

"Absolutely. If it means I get to be inside you." He nipped the section of skin on her nape that made her knees buckle. "If it means I get to touch you, and look into your eyes so you see how much I love touching you. See how much I love you."

Keely sniffled. "You are such a smooth-talking bastard."

"Guilty. But that's how you like me best. Will you turn around and look at me please?"

As soon as she did Jack was in her face.

"This kind of shit happens. And baby, we *are* married. We're immune to each other's bodily functions. So why did you freak out?"

"Because it's embarrassing. And probably makes you never wanna touch my tits again."

He cupped her breasts. "Wrong. I love your tits. It's just right now they've got a bigger purpose than entertaining me." He stroked his thumb over her nipple and she hissed. "See? You're sore from nursing. I tried not to rub against them because I won't add to your pain with something that's supposed to give you pleasure. I'll wait my turn until Piper is done with them." He ran his fingers along her collarbone and up her neck. "There are lots of other places on your body I love to touch besides your tits. I could show you if you'd like, sexy wife."

Keely started to cry again.

A panicked look crossed his face. "What did I say?"

"Exactly the perfect thing." She placed her hand over his heart. "How did I get so lucky that you fell in love with me? And you're still with me after my random bouts of craziness?"

He gave her a gentle, loving kiss as her answer.

She rested her forehead against his chest. "Sorry I ruined our sexy time."

"You didn't. We just had a break in the activities. Which is a good thing because my stamina sure isn't what it was two months ago."

"I don't care."

"So let's pick up where we left off, right here in the shower. That way if it happens again, we won't care. We'll already be wet."

Keely reached behind him and turned the water on.

Jack yelped when the cold hit his back.

But the water heated up. So did the kisses and the frantic touches between them.

Jack grabbed her ass and urged, "Jump up." Then he pressed her against the wall, using his body strength to hold hers in place. He locked his burning gaze to hers and impaled her. "God I love the look in your eyes when I do that."

"So do it some more." She raked her nails down his back. "And then do it some more again. Because we have a lot of time to make up for."

****

Two months later...at Piper's four-month checkup

"I hate bringing her to the doctor with all these sick people around," Jack said after they'd checked in at the clinic.

"Just keep the cover over her carrier and no one will bug her." But Keely chose seats in the corner just to be safe.

"Are you going to work tomorrow?"

"If I feel better." She'd caught a nasty flu bug in the last week that'd knocked her flat. Luckily she hadn't passed it on to either Piper or Jack. She'd made light of it, but it worried her because it'd lingered longer than normal.

Jack flipped through a parenting magazine before setting it aside with a sigh. "You sure you'll be okay while I'm gone? Because I can postpone the trip."

She grabbed his hand. "We'll be fine. We'll miss you, but our work lives didn't end just because we have a baby." Keely had returned to her rehab clinic last month. Two days a week she took Piper to work with her and on the full schedule days, Piper went to the daycare at Sky Blue, which should be renamed McKay daycare, since nearly all the kids were family members.

"I'm just having a harder time than I thought leaving you guys."

"Well, we are pretty damn cool."

Jack lifted a dark eyebrow.

"Pretty *darn* cool," she amended. They'd been trying to clean up their language around Piper, figuring it'd take them both two years to get a handle on it.

"Piper Donohue?" the nurse called out.

Jack picked up the carrier and they followed the nurse through the maze leading to the examination rooms.

After they were settled, Doc Monroe poked her head in. "I'm running behind today guys, if you want to see Griffin the PA, I'd understand."

"We'll wait," Jack said.

"Maybe you should run a flu test on me while we're waiting."

Doc Monroe came all the way into the room and scrutinized Keely. "Did you get a flu shot this year?"

"Yes."

"Typical flu symptoms?"

"Nausea. Headaches. I throw up, which is weird because I don't eat much. I'm clammy then I'm hot. Tired."

"How long has it been going on?"

"Over a week," Keely admitted and shot an apologetic look at her husband.

"We'll run tests so if you test positive we can offer Piper and Jack preventative treatment. I'll get you to the lab."

Keely had a blood sample taken. A urine sample taken. The worst one was the nose mucus sample. She slipped back into the exam room and sat next to Jack, who'd—big surprise—taken Piper out of her carrier and was holding her.

Piper grinned and kicked her feet at seeing her mama. Their daughter was beyond adorable—however she looked nothing like Keely or Jack with her dark red hair and big green eyes.

"Hey, beautiful girl. Those smiles are gonna disappear when they come in and stick you with needles."

"How many shots does she get today?" Jack asked.

"Three, I think." She rested her head on his shoulder. "I'm gonna miss you, GQ. Hurry back."

"I will. But you could give me something to remember you by tonight."

She lifted her head. "When did you start taking testosterone? Because you are as horny as a teenage boy lately."

Jack kissed her, sweet and slow and deep. "What can I say? My wife is smoking hot." He kissed her again. "Guys complain about their wives losing interest in sex after having a baby. But what do any of them do to fix it? If it's important it'll be a priority. It'll always be a priority for me. For us."

"I love that about you."

Another forty minutes passed and Keely was ready to climb the walls, even when Piper was content to sit on Daddy's lap and coo and babble at him.

Finally Doc Monroe swept in. "Sorry. Jack, why don't you get little miss stripped to her diaper so I can check her out." Then she looked at Keely and smirked. "Good news? Negative for flu. The other good news? You're pregnant." She set a big bottle of prenatal vitamins on the counter. "Congratulations."

"What?" Keely and Jack said simultaneously. "But how can that be?"

"What birth control measures were you using?"

"Well, none, but—"

Doc Monroe lifted her hand. "Please do *not* tell me you listened to that old wives tale about not being able to get pregnant while you're nursing."

Keely blushed. Then she whapped Jack on the arm. "I cannot believe you knocked me up again, Jack Donohue."

"Look at it this way. It's another first in the McKay family with your Irish twins." At Jack and Keely's blank looks, she clarified, "Two babies born within a calendar year."

Jack grinned and Keely whapped his arm again.

CHAPTER FOUR

Seven and a half months later...

"Come on, Keely, breathe."

"I am breathing, you bastard. Ow. Fuck. Goddamn that hurts."

Jack opened his mouth to remind her about language but Keely's death stare kept him quiet.

Swearing rules didn't apply during labor.

After the contraction ended, she reached for the towel only to have Jack already there, gently mopping her face. "Thanks."

"My pleasure." He kissed her temple. "This one seems to be going faster than the last one."

"Not fast enough for me," she grumbled.

"Hold on. Here comes another. Breathe with me."

When it ended, she panted, "Jack. They're getting worse."

"Want me to get the nurse?"

"Not yet."

As Keely waited for his cue for the next one, she had that same surreal sensation she had last year—the urge to flee. She needed to focus on something else. Her darling daughter.

Hard to believe Piper would be a year old in three weeks. Being two weeks early should've been an indication she'd do everything early. She'd walked at nine months and started talking at ten months. Of course her first word was *Daddy*.

"I know you're thinking about Piper. I texted your mom," Jack said. "She's fine. She's following Avery everywhere."

Since Cord and AJ's little girl Avery and Piper were nine months apart—same age difference as Keely and AJ—Cord and Jack already were already strategizing how to keep the girls from running wild.

Yeah, good luck with that, Keely's dad had told them.

"Keely, get ready."

The contractions came hard and fast. Time was divided in two: during a contraction and the break between contractions. She'd blocked much of her labor out last year. The pain had been unimaginable; she hadn't known how she'd survive it. And then soon as the baby popped out, pain gone. Completely.

But until that point? Hell. Which she was in right now.

The nurse came in and checked her. "Wow, lady, you're at nine."

"How can that be?" Jack asked. "Two hours ago she was at five."

"Second babies are quicker. Her body knows what to do. I'll get the doc. Get your scrubs on."

The next ten minutes were an exercise in control as Keely breathed through the need to push.

After Doctor Monroe arrived, and she could finally give in to that urge, it only took two tries and the baby was out.

Breathing hard, dizzy, hot, and sore, Keely still managed to sit up and look at the baby in Doc's hands. "Well?"

"It's a girl."

Jack laughed. "Next time I'm getting you pregnant in the summer so you don't freeze the stem off another one."

"Jack!"

"You know I'm kidding, cowgirl."

Then the blonde baby girl was placed on her stomach. Blonde? Where the hell had that hair color come from?

"Look at her." Jack murmured, "Hey, precious. Welcome to the family."

She screwed up her face and let out a loud cry.

"Healthy set of lungs on her." Doc Monroe cut the cord and the nurses whisked the baby away.

No, bring her back! I hardly got to see her.

"You were fierce in labor this time, beautiful wife of mine. I'm proud of you." He kissed her temple. "Thank you for adding another perfect girl to my life."

"I'm so happy that Piper has a sister." She sniffled. "I love my brothers, but after seeing how close my mom and my aunt are, I always wanted a sister."

"Maybe we'll provide them with a brother next time." He chuckled at her look of shock. "What? Carolyn kept birthing babies until she had a girl, so in some ways, it is a family tradition."

"You are reaching, buddy."

Doc Monroe walked over with the baby bundle. "She weighed in at seven pounds, fourteen ounces and she's twenty-three inches long." She handed Jack the baby. "What's her name?"

Jack looked at Keely. "Katie McKay Donohue."

The medical personnel picked up their stuff and they were gone.

"Let me hold her," Keely demanded.

"In a second."

"Are you gonna hog this baby too?"

"Probably."

****

Two months later…

Jack came up behind Keely and wrapped his arms around her, placing a kiss on the side of her neck. "Hi."

"Hi, yourself, handsome. What's up?" She rubbed her ass into his groin. "Besides your cock?"

He chuckled. "That's always your fault."

"The girls are down?"

"Mmm-hmm. Sleeping like the precious angels they are—until devil child Katie screams like a banshee and wakes them both up." Jack angled her head to the side and continued kissing her neck. "So we have a little time."

"To do what?"

"To mark the special occasion by getting naked."

"Oh? Are you talking about the *all clear from the doc to resume sexual relations with my husband* special occasion?"

"Not just that special occasion, smart mouth. Although that is a happy coincidence." He nuzzled the back of her head, breathing in the lilac scent of her shampoo. "I started the fireplace in the living room. Poured two glasses of red wine. Turned on a CD of that sappy goat-yodeling music you love so much."

"Geez, GQ. Did you roll out a bearskin rug too?"

"Damn. I knew I forgot something." He tugged on her earlobe until she hissed. "Come on, cowgirl. Let me be romantic and seduce you instead of throwing you on the tile right here in the kitchen and banging your brains out."

Keely faced him. Kissed him. Twined herself around him. "I prefer the hard bang after nine weeks and four days of no bang. But I'll indulge you and let you make sweet, sweet love to me. Let me grab the condoms."

Jack froze. "Condoms? Really?"

"Yes, really."

"But…I hate condoms. We haven't used them in years."

She drilled her finger into his chest. "Suck it up. No glove, no love. I'm not kiddin', Jack."

"How about if I pull out?" he asked hopefully.

Keely growled at him. "Do you want to get laid tonight or not?"

"Fine. Condoms it is."

Jack did an awesome job seducing her—if he did say so himself. Making her come twice before he got started on the main event. And yeah, it hadn't been too bad wearing a condom after Keely had used her mouth to put it on.

They both were too far gone, too desperate to reconnect for slow and steady to last very long. Each hard thrust into Keely's hot, wet cunt sent him closer to the edge. Her breathy moans in his ear. Each lift of her hips as she met him thrust for thrust. Then Jack was there, falling headlong into the hot wash of pleasure he only got from being body to body, skin to skin, heart to heart with the woman who owned him. The woman who loved him and gave him more joy in his life than he ever imagined possible.

After he'd regained his ability to think, and after he'd kissed Keely so thoroughly his cock was on board for round two, he eased out of her.

That's when Jack saw the condom had broken.

He must've worn a horrified look, because Keely pushed up on her elbows and said, "What's wrong?"

"Uh. You did get that condom on all the way, right?"

"For cryin' out loud, I know how to put on a...omigod the goddamned condom broke?"

"Apparently."

Silence.

Then Keely got right in his face. "So help me God if you got me pregnant *again* Jack Donohue, I'll—"

Jack gave her a smacking kiss on the mouth. "You'll what? Stop having sex with me? Not likely. You won't adore another baby like you adore the two beautiful babies we already have? Not likely."

"You are a sweet-talkin' man even after you got your pole polished? Wow. I'm one lucky broad."

He grinned. "You have to admit we've got this baby-making thing down."

"Well, practice does make perfect, and we've gotten in a lot of practice over the years."

Jack touched the side of her face. "Would you be upset if...?"

"Your supersonic sperm reached the goal once again?" Keely shook her head. "We tried to do the responsible thing. If it happens, it happens."

"So we can skip the condoms for round two?"

"Nice try, but not a chance in hell." She tossed him another condom. "This one is all on you." She kissed him and rested her forehead against his. "Happy anniversary, Jack."

"Happy anniversary, Keely."

Jack made love to her again. Slower. Sweeter. Wearing her out to the point she'd drifted off to sleep in his arms.

He didn't panic when he saw they'd broken another condom. He'd tell her later. For now he let her sleep. Chances were very good she'd need extra sleep in the coming months.

****

Seven months later...

"Piper McKay Donohue, get down from there right now."

"No!"

"I mean it. Get down."

"No!"

A chuckle sounded beside her.

Keely looked at her father. "Daddy, this is not funny."

"It surely is. Pipsqueak climbs everything like Cam did, but her defiant tone is all you, baby girl."

Piper started jumping on the couch. Her red pigtails bounced. The bells on her sock jingled, which made her giggle. A devious giggle if Keely had ever heard one. She pushed herself to get out of the recliner.

"Huh-uh. Stay put," her dad warned. "I'll get her." Grandpa scooped her up with one arm. "No jumpin' on the furniture, okay, Pipsqueak?"

"K." Piper squirmed to be let down. As soon as her feet hit the floor she made a beeline for the couch again.

Grandpa laughed and grabbed her, throwing her over his shoulder amidst her happy shrieks. "You are gonna be some trouble little miss." He walked over and deposited Piper on the floor. "Sit with your mama for a minute while I see what Gran-gran is doin'."

Piper scrambled onto the end of the recliner between Keely's knees and laid her head on Keely's enormous belly. "Hi babies."

Keely smoothed the damp ringlets from Piper's forehead. It was doubtful almost two-year old Piper understood the concept of babies inside the gigantic bump, but she said hi to the babies at least ten times a day anyway.

It'd come as a shock to learn she carried twins, especially so soon after Katie's birth. High blood pressure complications with this pregnancy meant she'd been on bed rest since the fifth month, which wasn't too bad since she wanted to be home with Piper and Katie anyway. Her family had pitched in to keep her company after Jack insisted someone be with her at all times. He'd cut back on his work schedule, so he was home at least part of every day. But today he'd had to drive into Rapid City for a meeting that couldn't be handled over the phone or via email.

Piper looked up at her. Those big green eyes—eyes just like Jack's—were serious and a little devilish. "What's that?"

She smiled. "My tummy is making some loud noises. Think the babies might be hungry."

"I hungry too."

"Go ask Gran-gran for a snack. But no cookies."

"K." Piper shot her mother a smug look before she leapt off the recliner and tore off into the kitchen.

Keely wiggled in the seat, trying to get comfortable. She felt heavier today like something had shifted down low in her abdomen. Movement made her nauseous so she hadn't done anything but sit for the last hour. Still, her heart raced like mad. Her fingers and toes tingled. Her shallow breathing increased the sensation of dizziness. This was not normal.

She put down the foot rest and set her feet on the floor. Had her toes fallen asleep? She couldn't feel the rug beneath her, just more of those sharp tingles.

Her mom came around the corner carrying Katie, who immediately started saying, "Mama, Mama, Mama."

"Hey, sweet pea."

Katie shrieked and pushed away from Gran-gran, reaching for Keely desperately as if she hadn't seen in her days, not minutes. Her mom set her down. Katie toddled over, her brown eyes teeming with tears, her blond hair sticking up in every direction. She clutched the side of the recliner. "Mama, Mama, Mama."

"I know it's naptime and you want a story, huh?"

Katie tried to crawl in her lap and Keely's heart about broke. Katie was such a sweet, snuggly baby, but Keely didn't have the strength to pick her up right now.

"Sweetheart? Are you okay? Your face is bright red."

"No. I'd better call Jack and have him get me to the doctor." A spike of pain hit her, like she was being ripped apart from the inside out. Then she felt a rush of wetness between her legs.

Alarmed, Keely looked down expecting to see water, but blood stained her shorts. Blood. A lot of blood. Oh God. Panicked, she stood abruptly.

Too abruptly. All the blood rushed from her head and she lost her balance. Black spots obscured her vision.

Her mom screamed, "Keely!"

Everything switched into slow motion. She knew she was going down but she couldn't make her arms work to break the fall.

Two strong arms caught her. "Whoa, girlie. I gotcha." But she and her dad both ended up on the floor anyway.

Keely couldn't breathe. Her belly started to cramp like she'd never felt. She groaned with pain. What was happening?

"Caro, call an ambulance."

Keely whispered, "No. Call Jack. Call him now."

"We will. But we've gotta get you to a hospital."

Her entire body shuddered with cold. Those swirling black and white spots were back. Her head felt like it was beneath a waterfall.

Yet she heard Katie crying. Hysterical I-want-my-Mama shrieks. Then Piper joined in. Keely needed to get to her children to calm them down, but she couldn't even move.

Rough-skinned hands stroked her face. "Stay still. Stay with me baby girl."

She opened her mouth but nothing came out.

"Caro, get the girls out of here," her dad said sharply.

The distressed cries of her daughters vanished.

Keely fell into a state of nothingness until the pain came again and her entire body convulsed from the power of it.

Voices rose and fell around her. She tried to concentrate on just one to pull her out of the void. Her dad's was the loudest.

"You are stayin' here," he snapped. "I'm ridin' in the ambulance with her."

"But Carson that doesn't make sense. She needs me—"

"Right now those little girls need you more. And sugar, you're close to hysterical. That ain't gonna help her. Jack's gonna need someone to calm him down and you're in no shape to do it."

"And you are?" she demanded.

"I have to be."

Loud noises, activity and more voices surrounded her. Then the world went black as Keely slipped into unconsciousness.

CHAPTER FIVE

After the phone call from Carson, Jack kept the speedometer at one hundred miles per hour as he drove from Rapid City to Spearfish. And Cam must've pulled some strings because no one stopped him.

He'd contacted Doc Monroe but she'd already gone to the hospital in Spearfish to consult on Keely's behalf. Then he'd talked to Keely's mom to make sure Piper and Katie were taken care of. Keely's sisters-in-law were on their way to take over so Carolyn could go to the hospital.

He glared at the dashboard clock. It'd been forty-five minutes since he'd received the call and he was still ten miles from Spearfish.

If anything happened to Keely he'd...

No. Don't go there. Just drive.

Everything became a blur until he arrived at the hospital.

He ran through the emergency room doors.

The nurse said, "Can I help you?"

"Keely Donohue. Arrived via ambulance from Sundance?"

She pointed to the door marked *Stairs*. "They can help you on the third floor."

He scaled the stairs two at a time. Before he reached the receptionist's desk, Carson approached him.

"How is she? Where is she?"

"They're prepping her for emergency surgery."

Jack had to brace his hand against the wall to keep his knees from buckling. "I want to be with her. I need to be with her."

"You can't be. Believe me, I asked."

Bullshit. The next medical person he saw would be taking him to Keely. "What happened?"

"She stood up, blood rushed out and she passed out. The EMTs didn't say much on the ride here." Carson cleared his throat. "Let's go to the surgical waiting area. Maybe they'll have more news."

The waiting room was empty, giving Jack room to pace. He went through a checklist of a dozen things he should've done. And two dozen things he shouldn't have done. Like get her pregnant again. It'd seemed funny and surreal, three pregnancies in three years. But he wasn't laughing about it now.

If she dies, it's your fault.

"God." He wanted to punch the fucking wall.

"Jack. Take it easy. You look like you're gonna pass out."

"That's because I can't fucking breathe until I know if she's all right."

A nurse in scrubs came into the room and Jack immediately loomed over her. "I want to see my goddamned wife. Take me to her now."

"Sir. Calm down."

"I will. Just as soon as someone tells me what's going on."

"The doctor will be out here to talk to you at some point."

At some point? Why were they being so vague about where Keely was? "Not good enough. I want answers now."

"Hold it together, son," Carson warned.

Jack set his hands on the nurse's shoulders. "I swear to Christ if something's happened to her and you people are—"

"Sir. Let me go or I'll have security remove you from the premises."

Shit. He hadn't even realized he'd grabbed her. He stepped back, embarrassed as well as angry. "Sorry."

But she'd already stormed off.

Then Carson was in his face. "This ain't helpin' anyone, least of all you. So sit the hell down and shut the fuck up."

Harsh words. Jack's response was just as harsh. "And you'd sit in the corner like a fucking lap dog if Carolyn was behind those goddamned doors?"

"No. I'd've already ripped the doors off the hinges. But I'm askin' you to be the better man than me, Donohue. Keely is gonna need you there by her side when she comes out of this."

If she comes out of it. If she's all right.

Carson poked him in the chest. "Get that look off your face. I will not allow myself to imagine anything but good goddamned news coming through those doors and you'd better not either." He paused. "Because I'm havin' a hard time breathing myself."

They stared at one another.

"Fine. I'll sit." That lasted for about five minutes. Jack got up and paced. His brain tossed out all sorts of fucked-up theories that he wished would just stop.

Carson stayed close by his side. When he wasn't staring aimlessly out the window.

Jack felt every single tick of the clock in a slow drip of time eating away at his patience.

It was the most excruciating sixty-seven minutes of his life.

The doors opened and he was on his feet before they closed.

Doc Monroe, in blue scrubs, stood next to another woman in blue scrubs.

"How is Keely?"

The other doctor said, "She had a placental abruption." Then she launched into an explanation of what it was and added that she suspected Keely had suffered from preeclampsia, which had Jack seeing red because he wanted to know how the fuck his wife was doing, not be subjected to a lesson on medical terminology.

Doc Monroe interrupted. "What Dr. Janis here, the OB who did the surgery, is getting at, is Keely is in recovery. We had to put her under for the emergency C-section."

"So she's...?"

Doc Monroe put her hand on his arm. "She's fine, Jack."

His relief wouldn't kick in until he saw her. "When can I see her?"

"She'll be in recovery at least another hour. Then we'll move her to a post-op room." The two doctors exchanged a look. "Don't you want to know about the babies?"

Christ. How had he forgotten? "Are they all right?"

"Baby boy one is having some breathing difficulties, but it's to be expected given his placenta detached. Baby boy two is perfectly healthy with no trouble whatsoever showcasing his lung capacity. The birth weights were in normal range for twins born at thirty-six weeks."

Carson clapped him on the back. "Congrats."

Jack still couldn't wrap his head around two babies and they'd had months to prepare.

"Would you like to meet your sons?" Doc Monroe asked.

"I have to see Keely first."

More exchanged looks.

"Sounds strange, I know, but I want to be with her when we see our babies for the first time." He ran his hand through his hair. "Is there any way I can stay in recovery with her until she wakes up? I promise I won't do anything but sit beside her."

"Jack—"

"Joely. Please. I'm dying here."

Her eyes softened. "I'll see what I can do."

Carolyn rushed in the room. "Tell me what's going on."

"Keely's in recovery and the babies appear to be fine." Carson wrapped an arm around her and pressed his lips into her hair. "We haven't seen them yet."

That gave Jack an idea. "Can I give them permission to go do all the baby stuff while I'm with Keely?"

Dr. Janis shrugged. "Your call, Dr. Monroe."

"I'm fine with it." She smirked. "Another first in the McKay family. Grandpa and Grandma get to meet the babies before the parents."

Jack finally allowed himself to smile.

****

Jack held Keely's hand. He only took his eyes off her to look at the monitor. Not that he understood what the lines meant but they hadn't changed, which was a good thing.

The nurse came in every ten minutes and checked her.

But Keely didn't stir.

He pressed her palm against his cheek, wishing she'd wake up and bitch at him for being too lazy to shave.

Time passed in a void, but he didn't have a sense of helplessness because he was with her. Didn't matter if she wasn't aware he was by her side.

Then her fingers twitched and he was instantly alert.

Keely opened her eyes. She blinked several times and cast a panicked glance around the room before seeing him. "Jack?"

"I'm here, baby." He shot to his feet and framed her face in his hands before he kissed her. Once. Twice. By the third time his eyes were wet. He whispered, "I love you."

"I love you too." Her confused eyes searched his. "Why are you cryin'? Did something happen to the babies?"

"No. They're both fine. I just..." He pressed kisses on her beautiful face. "It's been a rough day and I went half-crazy thinking I'd never get to say those words to you again. You scared the life out of me, Keely."

"I'm sorry."

"Don't apologize." He kissed her again—he couldn't seem to stop kissing her, touching her, breathing her in. "How are you feeling?"

Tears trickled from the corners of her eyes. "I hurt everywhere."

That was a punch to the gut. "I'll see if I can't get you a painkiller. But first I want to tell you..." Jack buried his face in her neck. "No more," he said hoarsely. "I don't care about the who-can-have-the-most-kids competition you've got going on with your crazy-ass baby-making brothers and cousins, but we're done. No more pregnancies. I can't—*I won't*—put you through this again. If anything happened to you, Keely, I'd..."

"Jack. I'm—"

"Let me finish. You are my world, you are my everything, and I'd never recover from losing you. Never. I don't think you understand—"

"I do understand; trust me, because I feel the same way." She touched his face. "Hey. I'm right here with you. I'm not goin' anywhere."

He lifted his head. "I've already talked to Doc Monroe about scheduling a vasectomy as soon as possible."

"You're serious."

"Completely. We have four kids and that's plenty. You went under the knife today so it's my turn to ensure that I never have to go through another day like today."

The nurse came in, checked her over, administered the painkiller and made arrangements to move her.

"So tell me about our boys. Weight, length, hair color."

"Ah...I haven't seen them yet."

Keely's tired eyes widened. "What? Why not?"

"Because you and I have this tradition of seeing our babies for the first time together, so I waited."

"That's so sweet. That's so...you." She motioned him closer for a kiss. "Thank you." She rested her forehead to his. "As anxious as I am to meet our sons, I'm really wrung out. Can we wait a little longer?"

"Of course."

Her eyes drifted shut but her grip on his hand tightened. "You'll stay with me?"

"Always."

****

Three hours later the nurses wheeled two bassinets into Keely's private room. "The baby with the blue tag around his ankle was born first." Then they left.

Keely scooted the head of the bed upright. "Does it give the birth info on there?"

"Yeah." Jack peered at the sticker. "This one was six pounds even. Nineteen inches long." He leaned over to look at the other sticker. "Wow. Exactly the same for this one."

"Okay, let's see 'em."

Jack gently placed the small bundles side by side on the middle of the bed and sat on the opposite end. "Unveiling on the count of three."

"One, two, three."

The light blue hats came off first. Jack laughed, looking back and forth between the babies. "Black hair. I'm surprised one's isn't black and the other's brown. Then we'd have every color of hair represented in the Donohue household."

"Not happening with identical twins, GQ."

During the barrage of tests Keely had endured, they'd learned the babies were identical. "So let's see how alike they really are."

The boys squalled when they were stripped down to their diapers. But Jack and Keely examined every inch of them. They looked at each other with complete bewilderment.

"How on earth will we ever tell them apart? They are identical in every way."

"Maybe we can have India give one of them a tiny tat so they can't pull the twin-switcheroo on us when they get older," Jack suggested.

Keely whapped Jack on the arm. "A tattoo?"

"I was joking."

"Good. 'Cause I was thinking we should have one circumcised and one not. That way we'll always be able to tell them apart."

"So when one of them comes home past curfew when he's sixteen, you'll stand on the porch and say, *drop your drawers, son, so I know which one of you to punish?*"

She laughed. "I guess that is a little ridiculous."

"How about if we just leave the blue band on Jack Jr. for a while?"

"That'll work." She wrapped up the baby closest to her and smooched his cheeks before snuggling him close. "JJ Donohue, you're gonna be a handsome sucker like your daddy. I just know it."

Jack wrapped up the other baby, the one without the blue band and tucked him into the crook of his arm. "So we're still naming him Liam?"

"Yep. But I'd like his middle name to be Carson. After all the grandsons my dad has, not one has been named after him. It's time."

"Daddy's girl to the core," he murmured.

"Speaking of girls..."

"Your mom promised she'd bring them tomorrow." Jack noticed Keely's frown hadn't gone away. "You starting to hurt again?"

"A little."

"But that's not it, is it?"

She shook her head. "How on earth are we gonna handle four kids? We're outnumbered."

"No idea."

"That's helpful."

Jack shrugged. "Just being honest. But the next eighteen years ought to be interesting."

Howdy Readers!

Thank you for following the McKays and Wests on another
Rough Riders adventure! If you're so inclined to spread the word
about the Rough Riders world, there are a couple of ways to
share the cowboy love:

Write a review

Pop over to Lorelei James on Facebook and like me
Follow Lorelei James on Twitter
Stop by Lorelei James website
Sign up for my Lorelei James newsletter – I promise I won't
inundate you with promo
Join the Lorelei James Gang on yahoo groups

About the Author

Lorelei James is the *New York Times* and *USA Today* bestselling author of contemporary erotic western romances set in the modern day Wild West and also contemporary erotic romances. Lorelei's books have been nominated for and won the Romantic Times Reviewer's Choice Award as well as the CAPA Award. Lorelei lives in western South Dakota with her family...and a whole closet full of cowgirl boots.

Rough Riders series:

Bk 1—Long Hard Ride

Bk 2—Rode Hard, Put Up Wet

Bk 3—Cowgirl Up and Ride

Bk 4—Tied Up, Tied Down

Bk 5—Rough, Raw, and Ready

Bk 6—Branded As Trouble

Bk 6.5—Strong Silent Type

Bk 7—Shoulda Been A Cowboy

Bk 8—All Jacked Up

Bk 9—Raising Kane

Slow Ride—free read

Bk 10—Cowgirls Don't Cry

Bk 11—Chasin' Eight

Bk 12—Cowboy Casanova

Bk 13—Kissin' Tell

Bk 14—Gone Country

Bk 15—Redneck Romeo – available June 18th 2013

Made in the USA
San Bernardino, CA
07 April 2014